P9-DMF-108

THE SECRET OF THE WOODEN LADY

ADVENTURE abounds on the *Bonny Scot* in Boston Harbor as Nancy Drew helps Captain Easterly uncover the mystery of his ghostly visitors. From the moment the clever young detective and her friends, Bess Marvin and George Fayne, take up residence on the old clipper ship they are confronted with fire, theft, and other dangerous situations.

Nancy faces an additional challenge: to find a clue to the clipper's missing figurehead. If she is successful, it will help her lawyer father to trace the history of the *Bonny Scot* and establish a clear title to the ship for Captain Easterly. But strangely there are no records of the *Bonny Scot's* past. Why? And why has the prime suspect in the recent robbery at Bess Marvin's home followed the three girls to Boston?

Join Nancy and her friends in their thrilling adventures and discover for yourself the romantic secret of the old sailing ship.

"Here it is!" Nancy cried out. *"Dream of Melissa—
all spelled out."*

NANCY DREW MYSTERY STORIES®

The Secret of the Wooden Lady

BY CAROLYN KEENE

ST. JOHN THE BAPTIST PARISH LIBRARY
2920 NEW HIGHWAY 51
LAPLACE, LOUISIANA 70068

GROSSET & DUNLAP
Publishers • New York
A member of The Putnam & Grosset Group

Copyright © 1995, 1967, 1950, by Simon & Schuster, Inc. All rights reserved.
Published by Grosset & Dunlap, Inc., a member of The Putnam & Grosset Group,
New York. Published simultaneously in Canada. Printed in the U.S.A.
NANCY DREW MYSTERY STORIES® is a registered trademark of Simon & Schuster,
Inc. GROSSET & DUNLAP is a trademark of Grosset & Dunlap, Inc.
Library of Congress Catalog Card Number: 72-90826 ISBN 978-0-448-09527-1

Contents

The Secret
of the
Wooden Lady

CHAPTER I

A Call for Help

"PLEASE call your father, Nancy," Hannah Gruen, the Drews' housekeeper, said. "Fried chicken is better when it's hot."

Nancy, her titian hair still damp from a swim, skipped lightly up the carpeted stairway and tiptoed into her father's den. She slid quietly onto an arm of his big green club chair and patted the top of the lawyer's head.

"Supper, Dad! Goodness, what's in that letter to make you frown so?"

Carson Drew laid the handwritten letter down on his desk and smiled up at his vivacious, eighteen-year-old daughter.

"Clipper ships and sea ghosts!" he replied. "I hope the man's not imagining things!"

"Who, Dad?"

"My old friend Captain Easterly—that interesting fellow we met in Boston last year. Remember?"

"Does he still live on that clipper ship in the harbor?"

"Yes. But he doesn't like the mysterious person who prowls around the old craft."

Nancy's keen blue eyes shot an inquisitive glance at her father. "Come on, Dad," she said impatiently, "let me in on the secret!"

Tall, handsome Carson Drew stood up, thrust his hands into his pockets, and paced the floor.

"It's a peculiar thing," he said.

Mr. Drew explained that Captain Easterly, who had rented his ship-home for a couple of years, had recently decided to buy it. At once things had begun to happen on shipboard. A mysterious prowler had made several visits and done a lot of searching, but apparently had never taken anything.

"Does Captain Easterly have any idea what the person was looking for?" Nancy asked.

"Not the faintest idea," the lawyer replied. "Some of the dockmen think the ship is haunted."

"Does Captain Easterly want us to solve the mystery?" Nancy asked eagerly.

The lawyer stopped pacing and looked at her, a twinkle in his eyes. "Easterly has asked me to come to Boston. He writes that the owner of the ship agreed to sell it, but when it came time to draw up a contract, his lawyer discovered that he doesn't have clear title to the property. Easterly had someone in Boston make a search, but no record of the previous owners could be found. The captain wants me to make a search immediately because he is eager to complete the purchase before the owner goes West."

"I see," Nancy said. "Is that all?"

"That's all for me," Mr. Drew replied. "But— how would you like to go to Boston with me and work on the mystery?"

"Wonderful, Dad!"

At that moment Hannah Gruen appeared in the study doorway. "Supper is getting cold!" she announced.

"Hannah, Dad and I have a new mystery to solve!" Nancy exclaimed.

"Mystery or no mystery, this family must eat," Hannah said firmly. "Come along."

Mr. Drew winked at his daughter and they followed the housekeeper downstairs to the dining room. Mrs. Gruen had taken care of Nancy and the Drew household since the death of Mrs. Drew many years before, and father and daughter were very fond of her.

"How soon will we be going to Boston, Dad?" Nancy asked when they were seated.

"Let you know in the morning. I have an appointment at my office at eight tonight. Want to drive me downtown? I'll walk back."

"Love to," Nancy said.

"And you can drop me off at my club meeting," Mrs. Gruen added.

Two hours later, driving home alone in her convertible, Nancy thought over the conversation she had had with her father. An old clipper ship with unknown former owners, and a mysterious prowler . . .

This was not the first time Nancy had been called upon to rescue someone in trouble. Ever since people had learned that Nancy possessed unusual ability to solve mysteries, the young detective had been called upon to track down scoundrels of various types. Only recently she solved the strange case of *The Clue of the Leaning Chimney*. Captain Easterly's present predicament seemed like the beginning of another case for Nancy.

As Nancy turned into her driveway, she heard the telephone ringing in the house. She parked the car and hurried into the hall to answer it.

"Nancy?" It was Bess Marvin, one of her best friends. The girl's soft voice was a bit quavery. "I'm all alone—Dad's at the council meeting and Mother's gone to visit Aunt Celia."

"Not afraid, are you?" Nancy teased. "I'm glad you called. I have some wonderful news."

Nancy excitedly related the story of Captain Easterly's clipper ship and how a mysterious person was looking for something aboard, maybe a hidden treasure.

"Dad's going to take me to Boston with him!" Nancy concluded.

"You'll probably have some exciting adventures, Nancy," Bess said. "But do be careful."

Nancy was about to put down the telephone when Bess cried out, "Nancy, wait!"

"What's the matter?"

"I hear someone upstairs." Bess's voice was a frightened whisper. "There *is* someone! Oh, Nancy!"

As Bess screamed, there was a clatter at the other end of the line as if she had dropped the telephone.

"Hello!" Nancy cried. "Hello! Bess!"

There was no answer. Nancy tried to call the police. The lines were busy! She put down the telephone, then ran out of the house and hopped into her car.

The Marvin home was only a few blocks away. Three minutes later Nancy parked at the curb and hurried toward the house. All the windows were dark. That was odd, she thought.

The great elm tree by the porch and the overgrown shrubs cast deep shadows on the lawn. Nancy thought she saw something move among the rhododendrons next to the porch steps, but she told herself it was just her imagination; the breeze was moving the leaves.

She was halfway up the walk when suddenly an arm gripped her shoulder. Someone whirled her around and forced her toward the convertible.

The arm was tight against Nancy's throat; a

man's arm in a rough coat sleeve, cutting off her breathing. His fingers pressed into her left shoulder. She caught sight of the short square hand, the broken nails, and on the little finger a ring which glimmered in the light from a street lamp.

She strained every muscle and tried to jerk free. The man brought his other hand up to the back of her neck. His thumb pressed unbearably. Nancy ceased to struggle.

When she opened her eyes, she was half lying, half sitting in the front seat of her car. There was no sound except the drone of locusts. Slowly Nancy regained full consciousness. The Marvin house was still dark. Where was Bess? Nancy realized she must get help. She must get out of the car.

With effort Nancy pulled herself upright, but her hands and legs seemed to be paralyzed. Somehow she must give an alarm!

She tried to scream, but her voice was weak and small. The horn! She leaned on it with her full weight and kept leaning. Someone surely would hear it.

Presently the front door of the house next to the Marvins' flew open, and a man's voice bellowed, "Shut off that horn!"

Nancy kept on blowing.

Mr. Beaman marched down his front walk,

*Someone whirled Nancy around and forced her toward
the convertible*

and strode furiously to the convertible. "What's the meaning of this?" he demanded.

Nancy managed a weak smile. "I had to do it, Mr. Beaman. Sorry. Can't get out of the car!"

Mr. Beaman leaned closer. "Why, Nancy Drew! Are you hurt?"

"I'm recovering. Got knocked out. Bess Marvin —I'm afraid something has happened to her."

"I'll get Mr. Simmons," Mr. Beaman said excitedly, not waiting to hear any more. "You sit still. Don't go into the house alone."

Nancy watched him hurry across the lawns to the Simmons' house. She was feeling stronger now, and was sure that the intruder, whoever he was, would not have stayed around to be caught. She stepped to the curb, then walked cautiously toward Bess's house.

Nancy had reached the porch steps when Mr. Beaman and Mr. Simmons came running across the grass. They swung the beams from their flashlights over the bushes and shrubs, but there was no one around.

"My wife is calling the police," Mr. Simmons said. "Say, you look pretty shaky, Nancy. Sure you're all right?"

"I'm fine," Nancy assured him. "Oh, I hope nothing has happened to Bess. Let's hurry."

They opened the screen door and entered the dark hall of the Marvin home.

CHAPTER II

The Telltale Ring

NANCY found the light switch and the three of them stood there a moment, blinking. There were no signs of a struggle in the hall. The telephone was back in place and the big bowl of peonies beside it was undisturbed.

"Bess!" Nancy called. "Bess, where are you?" There was no answer.

"You two look around down here and I'll go upstairs," Mr. Simmons suggested.

Mr. Beaman was already going through the first floor, switching on lights.

"Somebody's raised Cain up here," Mr. Simmons called down in a moment.

Mr. Beaman hurried upstairs. Nancy, left alone in the hall, had an idea. She reasoned that someone had come up behind Bess as she stood at the telephone. He probably had knocked her out. If so, where could he have concealed her?

As Nancy looked about, she remembered the deep closet back of the stairway. Nancy opened the door and peered into the darkness.

"Bess!" she called. "Bess!"

There was a murmur from behind the coats. Nancy shoved them aside and bent down. Bess was lying on the floor.

"Bess, are you hurt?" Nancy exclaimed, kneeling beside her friend.

The girl slowly opened her eyes. "I—I— What happened?"

"Somebody knocked you out," Nancy said. "Don't you remember?"

Bess sat up and cautiously rubbed the back of her head. "I saw him, all right. He came tearing down the stairs, holding a handkerchief over his face. Then he grabbed me around the shoulders and pressed his thumb into the back of my neck. Oh, it was awful!"

"The same man who overpowered me!" Nancy declared. "I wonder when he got into the house."

"While I was out," Bess replied. She was calmer now. "I drove with Mother to Aunt Celia's and walked home. I suppose the man didn't hear me come into the house, so he was trapped."

Nancy called to Mr. Simmons and Mr. Beaman.

"It was a thief, no doubt about it," Mr. Simmons told Bess. "You should see your parents' bedroom. Looks like the day after a hurricane."

He telephoned City Hall, got Mr. Marvin out of the council meeting, and told him to come home at once. A police car, its siren screeching, came up the street, and in a moment officers Kelly and Flynn walked in the front door.

"Nancy Drew on the job already?" Officer Kelly asked, smiling. "What's the trouble?"

They told him what had happened.

"Robbery?" Flynn suggested.

Mr. Beaman nodded. "Come upstairs and see for yourselves."

When they entered Mr. and Mrs. Marvin's bedroom it was obvious that someone had made a hasty and rather clumsy search for jewelry. Bess picked up a blue velvet box from the bed.

"Mother kept her valuable jewelry in this," she said. "A pearl necklace, some pins, and several rings."

"Does your father own a diamond ring, Bess?" Nancy asked suddenly.

"Yes. Why?"

"The man who pushed me into the car was wearing one on the little finger of his left hand."

"Can you describe the fellow?" Officer Flynn inquired, taking out his notebook.

Nancy shook her head. "He came up behind me—all I really saw were his coat sleeve and his right hand."

"He wasn't tall," Bess put in, "and he wore a baggy gray suit. I think he had on sneakers—he made hardly any noise."

While they were talking, Nancy was turning over in her mind the peculiar actions of the thief. It was easy to understand why he had wanted to get rid of Bess—undoubtedly he had heard her say she knew there was someone in the house. He did not want her to call the police.

But why had he taken such effective means to keep Nancy out of the house? she wondered. He already had stolen the jewelry and left Bess unconscious. Why didn't he escape?

Nancy thought she knew. He needed more time for something else. She got down on her hands and knees and began a search of the bedroom carpet, inch by inch.

"What are you up to?" Kelly asked.

"Just a hunch," Nancy told the officer.

Lifting the edge of the bedspread, she reached as far under the bed as she could. Nothing there. She went around to the other side and did the same thing. This time her hand touched a small, hard metal object.

"Nancy, you've found something!" Bess cried.

"Get me a sheet of your mother's stationery," Nancy requested.

Bess obeyed and Nancy carefully slid the paper under the object so as not to mar any fingerprints, and brought it out.

"A man's signet ring!" Mr. Simmons exclaimed. "Perhaps it belongs to Mr. Marvin."

Bess shook her head. "I've never seen it before. And the initial on it is F."

At that moment Mr. Marvin came running up the stairs. "Bess, are you all right?" he asked with deep concern. "What's going on?"

"I'm perfectly all right, Dad," Bess assured him. "I'm afraid most of Mother's jewelry has been stolen, and also your diamond ring. This isn't your ring, is it?"

Mr. Marvin glanced at it. "No."

"Then it was dropped by the thief," Flynn concluded. "But I can't understand why the fellow took off his ring here."

Nancy said she thought the thief had picked up the extension telephone to listen to Bess's conversation. While he listened, he had slipped his own ring off to try on Mr. Marvin's diamond. The signet ring had rolled off the telephone table and under the bed. Then he heard Bess say someone was upstairs, so he had to quiet her before she could call the police.

"Before he had a chance to hunt for the ring, I drove up to the house," Nancy went on. "So he knocked me out and came inside again. When I leaned on the horn a couple of minutes later, he fled, probably through the back door."

"Right," Kelly said. "It was open."

"Can you get any fingerprints from this ring?" Nancy asked the policeman.

Flynn shook his head. "All we can hope for are partial prints from such a small surface. But the initial may help. The design is unusual. Anyway, Miss Drew, you did a nice job of deduction."

The policeman took an envelope from his pocket and dropped the ring into it.

Nancy drove home, followed by the police car, although she did not think she needed their protection. The young detective felt sure that the man who had lost the ring was far from the scene of the robbery by this time. Perhaps he had even left River Heights.

Nancy thought about him as she put the convertible into the garage. Her father and Mrs. Gruen had not yet returned. She entered the house, climbed the wide stairs, and went to bed.

Somewhere, sometime, she had seen that man's right hand before. There was something different about it. What was it? Unable to find the answer, she fell asleep.

Early the next morning Nancy was awakened by a joyful bark outside her door. Togo, her terrier, wanted to come in. Nancy reached over and opened the door. Togo put his front paws up on the bed and barked again.

"Good morning, silly," Nancy said, grinning at him. "Togo, I have a big problem, but I'll get up in a minute and play with you."

Her thoughts returned to the puzzle of the night before. She recalled vividly the rough arm pressing against her throat, the hand gripping her left shoulder. The hand with broken nails and a diamond ring. The middle finger, she recalled, was unusually short.

Suddenly Nancy sat straight up. She remembered where she had seen a hand like that! It belonged to a man who had worked at Larry's service station.

She realized that it might not be the same man. Probably lots of people have short middle fingers. But it was a clue.

Nancy dressed quickly and hurried down to breakfast to tell her father and Hannah Gruen of the night's excitement. When she finished, Mr. Drew reached over and put his hand on his daughter's arm.

"Be careful, Nancy. This thief sounds like a person who might become extremely dangerous if he thought you were on his trail."

"Don't worry, Dad."

Mr. Drew folded his paper. "I think we'll take the midnight train to Boston tomorrow night. That all right with you, Nancy?"

"I'll be ready. You know I'm going up to Emerson to the dance tonight. I'll be back by noon tomorrow."

"Remember me to Ned," her father said, a twinkle in his eye.

As soon as breakfast was over, Nancy hurried out to the garage, jumped into her convertible, and drove to Larry's service station.

"Good morning," Larry greeted her. "What'll you have?"

"Fill it up," Nancy said. "And I want to ask you some questions, if you don't mind."

"Go ahead." Larry started filling the tank and listened while Nancy described the man who had once worked for him.

"You mean Howard Fay." Larry frowned. "We fired him two years ago. He was light-fingered, I thought, but I couldn't catch him with the goods."

"Do you know where he is now?"

"No."

Nancy thanked Larry and started the motor.

"By the way, his nickname was Flip," he shouted as she pulled away.

Nancy drove to police headquarters, went directly to Chief McGinnis, and gave him the information, along with her reason for thinking Howard Fay might be the man who had robbed the Marvins.

"Thanks very much, Miss Drew," the officer said. "Just one more debt this department owes you."

Before starting on her trip to Emerson College, Nancy stopped by the Drew home. She put a pale-green evening dress into her suitcase, which already was packed, and drove off.

The closing dance of the college year was a gala one, and good-looking, athletic Ned was unusually attentive. When the dance was over, Ned suggested that Nancy take a walk with him around the campus in the moonlight before returning to the cottage where she was staying.

"A last request for many a moon." Ned sighed.

"Why, what do you mean?" asked Nancy, laughing.

"Here you are off to Boston tomorrow on a ghost hunt," Ned explained, "and I thought we'd see a lot of each other before I left for my counselor job at camp."

"Oh, I'm sorry, Ned," said Nancy, "but Captain Easterly really needs our help."

"Well, I suppose you must go," Ned continued, "but I'll miss you."

"Look!" Nancy said suddenly. "Your camp isn't far from Boston. If you get a chance, why don't you stop at the hotel where Dad and I'll be staying?"

"Fine!" said Ned. "That ship's ghost is going to have competition when I arrive in Boston."

Happy but a bit weary due to the late hour, Nancy said good night, hoping to see him in Boston.

She arrived in River Heights the next morning at noon. As she carried her suitcase up to her room, Mrs. Gruen called:

"Good morning, Nancy. Someone's on the phone. I can't make head nor tail of what he wants."

Nancy picked up the telephone.

"I want Mr. Drew—Carson Drew," a voice said gruffly.

"He's not at home. May I take a message? This is his daughter."

"You'll do. Tell your father to stay away from Easterly's ship. Do you hear?"

"Yes, I hear. But why—"

"I said stay away from Boston and that clipper."

"Who are you?" Nancy demanded.

There was no reply. The instrument clicked and the connection was broken.

CHAPTER III

The Mysterious Clipper

NANCY telephoned her father at his office and repeated the mysterious message.

"His voice sounded so threatening, Dad. I'm afraid Captain Easterly may be in danger!"

"I believe we should take the next plane for Boston," Mr. Drew answered soberly. "Can you be ready by two-thirty, Nancy?"

"I'll pack for both of us right away."

She called to Mrs. Gruen and Nancy told her the plan.

The housekeeper shook her head. "Sounds dangerous to me. Stay close to your father, Nancy. A young girl like you traipsing after criminals—" Hannah hustled upstairs to see that Mr. Drew's clothes were properly packed.

The lawyer came home shortly to lunch and greeted his daughter affectionately. "The police have high praise for your detective work, Nancy.

They've been checking the movements of that gas-station attendant."

"Flip Fay?"

Mr. Drew nodded. "He had been boarding at the south end of town. But night before last he moved away in a hurry without leaving a forwarding address. Looks as though you've put your finger on the thief, Nancy!"

"But he's gone, Dad."

Her father smiled grimly. "Criminals, like bad money, have a way of turning up sooner or later."

The Drews were still at lunch when the doorbell rang. Mrs. Gruen hurried to answer it. Nancy listened, tense, then relaxed as she recognized the lively voices of her friends Bess Marvin and George Fayne.

Bess and George were cousins, but there any likeness ended. Bess, blond and pretty, had a penchant for second desserts and frilly dresses. She shared Nancy's adventures out of deep loyalty to her but was constantly fearful of the dangers involved.

George was as boyish as her name. Her hair was dark, her face handsomely pert. George wore simple clothes and craved adventure.

After greeting the cousins, Carson Drew folded his napkin and pushed back his chair. "I'll see you at the office at two-thirty, Nancy."

He left the house and his daughter joined her friends in the living room.

"Hypers!" George exclaimed. "Why was I left out of all the excitement night before last?"

Bess shivered. "You mean you wish you'd been knocked out?" she asked, horrified.

George laughed. "Any news of the thief, Nancy?"

Nancy told the girls about Flip Fay. They remembered him and the short middle finger on his right hand. They hoped this slight deformity would make it easy for him to be identified and caught.

"And now, let's talk about something pleasant," Bess begged. "George, show Nancy your necklace."

Bess's cousin smiled ruefully. "My godmother is so fond of me, she just won't believe I don't like jewelry."

George took a box from her pocket. In it on a fluff of cotton lay a dainty gold chain with a brilliant red pendant.

"Of course it's not a real ruby," said Bess. "But it's a wonderful imitation."

"Why don't you try it on, Bess?" suggested Nancy.

She undid the safety clasp and fastened the necklace around her friend's plump, pretty neck. Bess admired the effect in a mirror.

"If it were a real ruby, it would be worth thousands of dollars," she declared. "Rubies are among the most valuable jewels in existence."

"More precious than diamonds?" her cousin asked.

Bess nodded. "I read a book once about gems. It said that rubies from Burma are the most valuable of all, especially the ones called 'pigeon's blood.' That's the color, of course."

"If you don't want it, you ought to give Bess the necklace," Nancy told George. "Anyone who knows so much about rubies deserves to have one of her own. Even though it's an imitation."

George laughed. "Exactly what I had in mind. Bess, the necklace is yours."

"You may be sorry you gave it to me, but thanks."

Nancy told her friends of the proposed trip to Boston. After a brief visit, George and Bess helped her carry the suitcases to the convertible.

"I'll drive you and your dad to the airport," George volunteered, "and bring your car back."

It was not long before the girls were saying good-by. Mr. Drew and Nancy stepped into the waiting plane, and in an hour were in Boston.

Nancy and her father registered at a comfortable hotel near Copley Square and taxied at once to the wharf where the three-masted *Bonny Scot* was tied up.

Captain Easterly, they were relieved to learn, was safe and in excellent health. He was delighted to see them, and proceeded at once to show them his unusual "home," with its main deck, and quarters and mess for officers and crew.

Nancy marveled at the intricate passageways, the efficient galley, and the homelike atmosphere of the ship. The captain's cabin was richly paneled in oak. Fastened on the walls were carved figurines.

"I think your ship is fascinating," Nancy told him as they seated themselves under an awning on the deck. "And it's so large. I hadn't any idea—"

The retired sea captain smiled proudly. "The *Bonny Scot* is not an unusually large clipper. But she's sturdy enough to sail around the world!"

Mr. Drew told him about the mysterious telephone call they had received in River Heights. "Do you know of anyone who might have a reason for trying to dissuade me from coming here?"

Captain Easterly raised his shaggy eyebrows. "No," he replied thoughtfully. "Mr. Farnsworth is the only person who knew that I had asked you to come. He'd have no reason to keep you away. In fact, he'd be the first one to welcome you. He's just as eager as I am to have this matter of title cleared up."

The elderly man leaned back in his chair. "Mr. Farnsworth inherited the ship from an uncle who bought it without a clear title. He has no papers telling about the early owners. And Farnsworth's not the man to spend money to prove anything.

So he's about decided to drop the whole idea of selling me the ship. Wants me to keep on renting her."

"And you don't want to do that," Mr. Drew put in.

The captain's blue eyes blazed. "I've decided to buy her, and I mean to buy her!"

"And I don't blame you a bit!" Nancy declared. "I love the *Bonny Scot* already."

Captain Easterly was obviously delighted to have such an enthusiastic audience. While the setting sun played warmly on the ship's deck, he pointed out the ways in which his clipper differed from the fishing schooners that were moored nearby.

"A clipper is square-rigged," he said. "The way I figure, she's got prettier lines than a schooner. I reckon you'd say she's more streamlined. Notice her long prow."

"Didn't most clipper ships have figureheads on their prows?" Nancy asked.

The captain smiled. "That's a good question. The *Bonny Scot* used to have a figurehead. You can see where it was fastened, right here under the bowsprit."

"What became of it?"

"That's one of the mysteries about this ship. The figurehead must have been lost or destroyed a long time ago. I'd certainly like to have it, or at least a duplicate. But nobody seems to know what it was—a man, or a—a wooden lady." He smiled.

Carson Drew turned to his daughter. "Now there's a project for you, Nancy. Find out what the clipper's figurehead looked like. After you've cleared up the mystery of the ghostly visitor, that is. Has he bothered you lately, Captain?"

"I'm away from the ship a good bit," Captain Easterly explained. "A couple of times, on my way home at night, I've seen a light moving aboard her. Saw it last night, as a matter of fact. But so far neither I nor the dockhands have been able to catch sight of anyone."

He looked quizzically at Nancy. "Young eyes are keener than old ones. If you care to spend some time on board, young lady, perhaps you'll be able to see the intruder."

Nancy's pulses quickened. "May I really? I'll be here tomorrow!"

"If I'm not around when you arrive, don't be alarmed. I'll likely be out buying provisions. Just amuse yourself till I get back. It won't be later'n eleven."

Carson Drew and his daughter left. On their way to the hotel, Nancy talked enthusiastically about the clipper ship.

"I'm sure the *Bonny Scot* has a wonderful history. If we only knew more about it. And Captain Easterly is a dear! He's so hospitable."

Carson Drew's eyes were sober. "The man

doesn't seem to realize that there may be danger aboard. We must get to the bottom of this quickly, Nancy, but with caution."

The next day, Mr. Drew left their hotel soon after breakfast to start his search for legal data relating to the ship's title. He planned to meet his daughter aboard the *Bonny Scot* at eleven o'clock.

As Nancy hurried toward the waterfront, she kept turning the mystery over in her mind. Why did the unknown visitor return again and again? Was he hunting for money or jewelry? Were there valuable papers hidden aboard?

The *Bonny Scot* rocked rhythmically alongside the wharf, majestic and peaceful. Nancy nodded to a dockhand and went aboard. Captain Easterly was not at home.

Nancy began to explore various parts of the ship. It was an eerie experience to be there alone in the stillness of the old vessel.

"Whoever comes here wants something desperately. He'll keep coming back until he finds it. If I could only think of some way to trap him!" she thought.

Suddenly Nancy stopped at the foot of the main companionway. Someone was not far off—someone moving very softly.

CHAPTER IV

A Ghostly Prowler

HER heart pounding, Nancy slipped into the shadows and waited for the footsteps to come nearer.

She thought the intruder might come along the main companionway. In that case she would have a chance to see his face!

The young detective held her breath. The footsteps ceased abruptly. Although she waited for half a minute, there was no further sound.

Nancy's better judgment told her not to allow herself to be trapped. She rushed up the companionway to the deck. There was the sudden squeak of oarlocks. Peering over the rail, she was in time to see a man in a rowboat pulling steadily away from the far side of the *Bonny Scot*. Was he the one who had been aboard, or an accomplice?

He wore soiled dungarees and a faded blue shirt. His lined, weather-beaten face and his grizzled beard told Nancy that he was not young, but he rowed with deep, powerful strokes and his little boat moved quickly away from the clipper.

The man must have felt her eyes following him, for he suddenly looked up and caught sight of her. With an angry scowl he redoubled his efforts. He would soon be out of sight among the small craft in the water.

Nancy ran ashore and approached two men who were pushing off in a small motorboat.

"Please take me," she begged. "I want to follow that old sailor in the rowboat. I think he's been trespassing on the *Bonny Scot.*"

"Sorry, lady." One of them shrugged.

"But he may be a criminal," Nancy pleaded.

"If he's a criminal, it's none of our business," the other man told her. "Go tell the police."

They started their motor and put-putted out into the choppy water.

Nancy looked quickly about her. There was no one else going out. Disappointed, she walked back toward the clipper.

She glanced at her watch. It was almost eleven o'clock. Her father would be along in a few minutes. As she stood on the pier, a taxi drew up and Mr. Drew stepped from it.

He smiled as his daughter hurried to meet him. "Is the captain on board?"

"No," Nancy said. "I suppose he'll be along

soon. . . . Dad," she whispered, "I think I've seen Captain Easterly's mysterious visitor!"

"You work fast. Where is he?"

Nancy told him of her suspicions. "But maybe it wasn't the old man after all. The 'ghost' may still be on board."

Cautiously father and daughter searched but found no one on the clipper.

"It must have been that man in the rowboat," Nancy declared. "But how did he get off the ship? There's no rope ladder hanging down, and he didn't use the gangplank."

Mr. Drew looked thoughtful. "You've got a real mystery to solve, Nancy," he said. "At least we know that the captain isn't seeing ghosts."

"What luck did you have, Dad?" Nancy asked. "Anything new on the ship's title?"

The lawyer shook his head. "It's going to be more difficult to trace than I had expected, I'm afraid. But I have a lead."

"What is it?" Nancy asked eagerly.

"I'm going to New Bedford. There's a very old shipbuilding firm there. I've been told that this company is a gold mine of information."

"Then maybe you'll find out something about the former owners of the *Bonny Scot*," Nancy said hopefully. "Dad, you might even find a drawing of her figurehead for Captain Easterly."

"Hope so." Mr. Drew took a steel tape measure from his pocket. "I'll need measurements of the ship if I'm going to describe her to the gentlemen in New Bedford."

Nancy helped him, running back and forth across the deck, calling out feet and inches, while he made notes of the ship's dimensions. They had almost finished when Carson Drew clapped his hand to his coat pocket. "I almost forgot a telegram that came for you, Nancy. I picked it up at the hotel."

Nancy ripped open the yellow envelope. "Why, Dad," she said, "Bess and George are coming to Boston to stay with me! They'll be here today— on the one-thirty plane. That's wonderful. But what in the world—"

Suddenly Nancy caught the twinkle in her father's eyes. "Dad, you sent for them!"

Mr. Drew nodded. "The minute I knew I had to go out of town, I phoned the Marvin home. I wouldn't want to leave you alone while I'm in New Bedford."

"You think of everything, Dad." Then Nancy smiled. "I wonder how Bess will like our ghost. I can't wait to show the girls the *Bonny Scot*."

"Keep your eyes open, Nancy," her father advised. "Learn all you can, but be careful." He pocketed the tape measure and looked at his watch. "I'm afraid I can't wait for the captain. I must hurry to make the New Bedford train. And promise me you won't go down into the hold alone."

"Promise."

Expecting Captain Easterly any minute, Nancy wandered around for a while, in sight of the workers on the wharf. Still the captain did not come.

"I think I'll look over his books," she told herself. "Maybe I can learn something about figureheads."

She went below to the captain's cabin, and almost immediately discovered a worn volume dealing with early American sailing ships. She dropped into one of the armchairs and began to read.

"Ancient shipbuilders," the author stated, "looked upon the figurehead as a protector. The bow of the early fighting ship was very high and extended beyond the hull so that it could be run over the deck of another vessel. This allowed the sailors to jump off onto the decks of the enemy's ships.

"Even when the figurehead was no longer supposed to be a guardian in battle, the sailors thought of it as a great protection in storms. If the figurehead was removed from a vessel, often the men refused to sail."

Nancy wondered if Captain Easterly felt that way about his lost figurehead—as if the ship were without a protector. She put the book back on the shelf. "Anyway," she told herself, "I'll help the captain find out what the figurehead looked like."

The shining brass hands on the ship's clock in the cabin were creeping toward one. Nancy jumped up, hurried ashore, and hailed a taxi.

The driver had just pushed down the meter flag when Nancy noticed a green taxi pull away from the opposite curb. The green cab gathered speed. As it passed them, Nancy caught a fleeting glimpse of the occupant.

He looked like Flip Fay!

"Follow that taxi!" Nancy ordered, leaning forward.

Her driver sped through the heavy traffic, skillfully keeping the other car in sight. As Nancy's taxi drew close, the man in the back seat half turned around. He knew she was following him!

He must have told his driver to shake Nancy's cab, because suddenly the green one darted into a side street. The traffic light turned red. Nancy fumed at the wait.

The instant the light was green again, Nancy's taxi turned the corner to follow Flip Fay. But the green cab had disappeared.

"Sorry, miss," the driver said to Nancy. "I'm afraid we lost 'em."

"Never mind. Go on to the airport."

As she entered the waiting room, Bess and George were just coming through the gate, followed by a porter with suitcases.

"Nancy!" cried Bess, hugging her friend. "We

thought you'd be so busy with your mystery you wouldn't come to meet us."

Nancy laughed. "That almost happened. Guess whom I just saw in a taxi?"

"Not the ghost?" George inquired facetiously.

"Flip Fay—at least I think it was."

"In Boston?" Bess shuddered. "Oh, dear, maybe he'll knock us out again, Nancy!"

Bess went on to say that the police felt sure Flip was the thief who had broken into her house. But he did not have a police record.

"Maybe he's running away to sea," George remarked. "He'd be safe from the police. I'm dying to see the clipper," she went on. "Have you found any clue to the captain's mysterious visitor?"

Nancy told the girls about the footsteps and her suspicions about the grizzle-bearded sailor.

"Oh, Nancy," Bess exclaimed, "weren't you frightened?"

George reminded her cousin that it took more than an old grizzle-faced stranger to frighten Nancy Drew.

"Let's have a snack at the hotel, and then I'll take you ghost hunting," Nancy suggested.

When they reached the girls' hotel, Nancy picked up the room telephone and put through a long-distance call to the police chief in River Heights. She told him she thought Flip Fay was in Boston. Chief McGinnis thanked her and said he would get in touch with the Boston police at once.

"Shall I wear the ruby pendant George gave me?" Bess asked, trying the effect with a pink suit.

"Wear a ten-carat diamond, only let's get started," George urged.

Bess snapped on the necklace and they all went down to the hotel coffee shop for a light lunch. Twenty minutes later they got into a taxi. On the way to the dock, they did some further speculating about Flip Fay.

"Do you suppose he's the man who called your house and told you to stay away from the *Bonny Scot?*" Bess asked. "If he is the one, Nancy, you may be in danger."

Nancy was thoughtful. It was possible that Flip Fay had found out she had told the police he was the thief. If Fay were trying to leave the country from Boston, naturally he would not want her and Mr. Drew in the city.

"I don't see why Flip would be interested in the clipper," George spoke up. "There's no connection that we know of."

"We don't know very much of anything yet," Nancy reminded her. "As soon as you've seen the ship, I want to do a little investigating along the waterfront. Maybe I can find someone who knows Flip, or at least has seen him."

"What about old Grizzle Face?" George put in. "Are you going to try to find him?"

Nancy said this was her intention, and she laughed at George's nickname for the old sailor. The girls left the taxi and walked along the quay toward the clipper.

"What do you think of her?" Nancy asked proudly. "Isn't she a beauty?"

The girls admired the trim black hull of the *Bonny Scot* and hurried aboard eagerly.

Nancy, sure that the captain would be back by this time, took the girls to his cabin. He had not arrived. The cousins looked around, admiring the carved figurines on the walls. Bess especially liked the figurine of the Puritan maid.

"I'll bet she could tell lots of stories about this old ship if she could speak," Bess mused.

"Let's go ashore and inquire about Grizzle Face," Nancy suggested. "We can come back later to see Captain Easterly."

They strolled past interesting shops filled with ship's supplies—lanterns, compasses, calking cord, hardtack, fishing nets, and lines. Nancy stopped to speak to several longshoremen, and she also inquired in some of the shops and shipping offices, but no one could give her any information about either Flip Fay or Grizzle Face.

"My feet hurt," Bess groaned. "Let's sit down."

"There's a museum," Nancy said. "Let's go in. Maybe we'll see some figureheads; even the one from the *Bonny Scot*."

She led the way, and was delighted to find a

long room lined with carved figures from old ships. The attendant, Donald Blake, was glad to tell the girls something about his treasures.

"This young lady," he explained, "sailed around the world ninety times, it's said. That's better than most sea captains do!"

The face of the figurehead was calm and composed. "She's ridden out storms and maybe even battles without a qualm!"

"This man looks like a pirate," George remarked, pointing to a fierce-looking, mustached figure, wearing a cocked hat and a sword.

"Good guess," said Mr. Blake. "He came from a Spanish pirate ship."

Nancy told Mr. Blake about the lost figurehead of Captain Easterly's clipper. "You don't happen to know anything about it?" she asked.

"I don't," Mr. Blake answered. "But this book may give us a clue."

He picked up a heavy volume from a desk and thumbed through the index.

"No *Bonny Scot* listed," he said. "Do you know when and where she was built?"

"So far we haven't found out," Nancy replied.

"Her figurehead may not even be in existence," Mr. Blake warned. "Some of the early American figureheads rotted away because the woodcarvers used soft wood instead of hard elm or oak.

"At times a crew would remove the whole

figurehead if they were afraid she'd be battered to pieces in a roaring sea," he continued. "Those old-timers thought a great deal of their wooden ladies. Well, I hope Captain Easterly finds his figurehead."

The girls thanked him and returned to the ship, hoping to see the captain. But the clipper was still deserted.

"I wonder what can be keeping him." Nancy frowned. "He said he'd be here this morning."

"Let's go somewhere and have a nice cold soda while we're waiting," Bess begged.

"I agree with you!" said George.

"You two go," Nancy decided. "I'll wait here."

George did not think they ought to leave Nancy alone on the ship. "Too many strange things are going on," she said, "and after all we came to Boston to protect you."

"I'll be perfectly all right," Nancy assured her.

The girls left. Nancy looked about the captain's cabin, once again admiring his orderly housekeeping: the gleaming brass hinges on the mahogany wardrobe, the bunk neatly made up and covered with a blue homespun spread. She noted a flashlight and a book on the little shelf over the bunk and saw that Captain Easterly, too, had been reading about figureheads. She reached for the book, then paused.

Had she heard someone on board? Captain Easterly? . . . No. . . . Nancy decided she had imagined the pad of footsteps. She took down the book and leafed through it.

The volume was titled *The Ten Greatest Pirates of History*. Nancy stopped at the chapter about an Indian Ocean ruffian who maintained a spy ring in the leading ports of the Orient. His underlings, the story said, learned about rich shipments of cloth and precious stones and would send messages to the pirate chieftain. Then the brigands would lie in hiding in some secluded island cove, waiting for their prey.

Nancy wondered whether the *Bonny Scot* ever had had such a misadventure.

Again Nancy thought she heard a noise and strained her ears to listen. "The pirate story is stirring my imagination," she thought.

Suddenly Nancy froze, her spine prickling. *There was someone behind her!* Someone had come softly along the passageway and into the cabin.

Nancy whirled, but before she could see the person, a coat was thrown over her head and powerful hands pushed her into a closet and slammed the door.

Mark of a Thief

NANCY tore the coat from her face. She was in a
small dark space, surrounded by clothing or
hooks and hangers. It must be the captain's ward
robe, she thought, as she tried to force the doo
open. It would not budge.

She could hear the intruder moving quickl
about the cabin, upsetting things, careless nov
of the noise he made. If only she could catch
glimpse of him!

Nancy put her eye close to the keyhole, but th
ey was in the lock and she could see nothing bu
a glint of light. She began a careful search of th
floor panels for some tiny crack through whic
he might watch the man's movements.

At last she found one—a small hole halfway u
the right panel where someone had driven a nai
Nancy glued her eye to the tiny opening an

waited with bated breath for the prowler to cross her line of vision. When he did, Nancy gave a little gasp.

Grizzle Face!

He had a chisel in his hand and began forcing the lock of one of the desk drawers. The fine wood splintered. Seizing the drawer, the man dumped its contents upon the floor. Then he did the same to the other two drawers. What was it he hoped to find?

Whatever the sailor wanted, it was not in the drawer. He abandoned the heap of things he had dumped out and began to explore the polished oak wall next to it. His big hands passed quickly over the wood, pressing here and there. Was he looking for a secret spring which would open one of the panels?

Then, as suddenly as he had come, Grizzle Face left. The cabin was silent. Nancy waited, wondering if he would return. Perhaps he had gone for an accomplice.

"Or he's searching in another part of the ship," she said to herself.

Once more Nancy tried to force the door. It was heavy, and her only reward was a bruised shoulder. The air was becoming bad, too.

In a moment she sighed with relief. She had heard two familiar voices. Bess and George were coming down the companionway! She shouted and pounded on the wardrobe door.

"Nancy!" Bess cried in a panic. "Where are you?"

"I'm locked in the wardrobe," Nancy answered, but George had already turned the key to let her out.

"Hypers!" George breathed. "Who locked you in here?"

"Grizzle Face, and look what he did to Captain Easterly's desk!" Nancy said, pointing to the heap of assorted articles from the drawers. "He's searching desperately for something—he even felt along the wall as if he hoped to find a secret panel."

Nancy said she was sure he had been frightened off the clipper by the approach of the cousins.

"Then why didn't we see him?" Bess countered, edging toward the door.

Nancy reminded her of the mysterious exit of the old fellow that morning. He had probably left the same way.

"And I'm going to find out where the place is," Nancy determined.

"Not now," George suggested. "Let's investigate this cabin. Do you suppose there *is* a secret panel?"

"Oh, come on," Bess pleaded. "We can return in the morning, and Captain Easterly will be here to protect us," she urged.

"Why don't you go ashore and wait?" George suggested. "Nancy and I want to see if there's anything to this secret-panel idea."

Bess hesitated. She did not want to stay on the clipper, yet she did not like the idea of being thought a poor sport. Suddenly she had an idea. She would ask the dock guard to come aboard. Without telling the others her plan, Bess left the cabin.

George and Nancy continued their search. George had taken off one of her sandals and was tapping along the wall with it.

Bess had been gone only a minute when there came a bloodcurdling scream. Nancy and George rushed into the passageway and around a corner. Bess was huddled against the wall, shivering with fright.

"Oh, Nancy," she whispered, "a head came right up through the floor!"

"What?" George exclaimed in disbelief.

"It did. I saw it."

"Where did you see it, Bess?" Nancy asked quietly.

"Down there, in the middle of the passageway." Bess pointed a shaking finger.

Nancy and George went to the spot and bent over to examine the floor. Nancy discovered a small hatch with an iron ring. She and George lifted it, despite Bess's fearful protests.

"There's a ladder," Nancy said excitedly. "It's an escape hatch leading from the hold. If we're going down, we'd better have a flashlight."

"Nancy, you're not going down there!" Bess screamed. "He's there! I know he is!"

"That's what we want to find out," Nancy told her firmly.

She already was hurrying back to the captain's cabin, where she grabbed the flashlight from the shelf over the bunk, and then joined the others.

"Come on, George," she said, starting down the narrow wooden steps.

"What am I supposed to do?" Bess wailed.

"Stand guard here," George told her.

Bess, not in the least comforted by this thought, decided to go with the others. Nancy, who was in the lead, stopped on the steps and swung her flashlight over the rough planking at the foot of the long, steep ladder. They could see some kegs and barrels, an oil drum, and a packing case.

There were plenty of places, Nancy decided, where a man could hide. It was completely dark, and the flashlight in her hand illuminated only a small space. She descended slowly, careful not to proceed until she was sure no one was hiding underneath the ladder.

The three girls reached the bottom of the steps. Staying close together, they began to work their way among the cases and barrels and coils of rope. After a while Nancy became convinced that there was no one else in the hold. George must have reached the same conclusion, for she said:

"Nancy, he got away. I'm sure he's not down here."

"I wish we could be sure," Bess said weakly.

The girls quickly investigated as much of the cluttered space as they could without climbing over the stacked-up articles, but they found no trace of the intruder.

Then Nancy went forward alone. "Here's the answer," she called, swinging her light over another ladder which led up to the lower deck. "He escaped through this hatch."

The three girls hurried to the deck and went ashore. Nancy walked over to a warehouse guard lounging against a wall.

"Did you see a man come off the clipper a few minutes ago?" she asked.

"Sorry, girls." He shook his head. "I haven't seen a soul. Has the captain been telling you his ghost stories?"

"Captain Easterly is a truthful man," Nancy said loyally. "I saw the intruder myself—twice. He is about sixty, and has a grizzled beard."

The watchman gave Nancy an odd look from under his black eyebrows. "I never saw anybody of that description around here, young lady. You a friend of Captain Easterly?"

Nancy said she was, and hurried away before he could ask any more questions. The girls found a taxi and went straight to the hotel.

Bess threw herself on the bed and breathed an

immense sigh of relief. "Am I glad to get away from that horrible old ship!" she said. "No more mystery today!"

After dinner the three girls went to a movie. Nancy was surprised that her father had not returned. He was not back by morning, either. Bess had lost her fright of the day before. The clear, warm day seemed to give her courage. After breakfast the three girls returned to the harbor.

They boarded the *Bonny Scot,* expecting to find Captain Easterly. Nancy shouted a "hello" into the interior. The only reply was the slight creaking of the vessel.

The captain's morning paper, neatly folded, lay on the deck where it had been pitched by a delivery boy.

"Maybe something has happened to him in his cabin. I'm going down and take a look," Nancy declared.

"Please don't," pleaded Bess, whose apprehension had returned. "Let the police investigate this."

"If anything's wrong with the captain, he needs us immediately," Nancy reasoned, hurrying down the companionway.

She found the door to his cabin standing open. The girl was shocked at the sight that met her eyes.

The captain's bunk was torn apart, and the drawers beneath it had been forced out and splintered. The wardrobe door gaped open and clothing was strewn about the room. An old chest looked as though it had been hacked with an ax, and there were great gashes in the beautiful paneled walls.

"Oh, Nancy," Bess gasped, "who would do such a horrid thing?"

George shook her head. "The captain will be terribly upset when he sees this. Old Grizzle Face must have come back during the night."

"I'm calling the police right now," declared Nancy.

Detectives Mallory and O'Shea of the Boston Police Department arrived promptly. With thoroughness and efficiency they examined the damage in the captain's cabin, and investigated the entire ship looking for some clue to the vandal. In the meantime, the girls straightened up Captain Easterly's quarters as best they could.

Finally the detectives returned and summed up the situation. Detective O'Shea said, "There's been unlawful trespass and considerable property damage, that's plain. Whether there's been robbery, too, only the captain himself can say. Know when he'll be back?"

Nancy told the officer she had not heard from the captain for two days. "My father and I were to meet him here yesterday morning. But Captain Easterly didn't appear."

"Know where the captain can be reached?"

"Who would do such a horrid thing?" Bess gasped

Nancy shook her head, frowning. "I honestly don't think he expected to be away. He was very anxious to have my father—he's a lawyer—trace the ship's title. He'd surely want to keep the appointment."

"And another thing, Captain Easterly knew someone had been coming aboard the *Bonny Scot* secretly. He wouldn't leave it unguarded— the whole night."

Mallory's eyes narrowed. "Think there's been foul play, Miss Drew?"

"I hope not," Nancy said earnestly. She told the officers about the anonymous telephone call to her father in River Heights, warning him to stay away from the clipper ship. She also spoke of the mysterious sailor who had pushed her into the wardrobe.

"Describe him, please," O'Shea requested.

"We call him Grizzle Face," George put in.

Nancy gave the detectives a detailed description of the sailor in dungarees. "Whoever he is," she added, "he must be looking for something of great value. That's why I'm worried about Captain Easterly."

"You mean you think the skipper has been kidnapped?" Bess asked excitedly.

Detective Mallory frowned. "Let's stick to facts, girls. Is there any other information you can give us?"

Nancy, wondering if Flip Fay might be involved in any way, asked if they had been notified that the robbery suspect might be in Boston. O'Shea said he had seen the report on Fay.

"Do you know him?" Mallory inquired.

"We all do," Nancy said. "He used to work at a service station in River Heights."

"Why don't we give you girls a ride to police headquarters?" O'Shea suggested. "I think the lieutenant would like to talk to you."

"Nancy, you can tell the lieutenant everything he wants to know," Bess suggested. "We'll do some sightseeing and meet you at lunchtime."

They settled on a restaurant in the center of the city. George and Bess left for a tour of the historic spots in Boston, and Nancy accompanied the detectives to headquarters to meet Lieutenant Hennessy.

At the lieutenant's request, Nancy recounted once more the strange events which had taken place in River Heights before she and her father had come to Boston. She also described Flip Fay as accurately as she could.

"Anything else?"

"Fay dropped a ring, which I found after the robbery and gave to the River Heights police. There was a strange F on it."

"Strange?" Hennessy repeated.

"Yes, it looked like—" Nancy searched her mind for the right word—"like a crow's foot."

Hennessy's eyes widened. "Did you say a crow's foot?"

"Yes."

The lieutenant went to a file of records, pulled out a folder, and handed Nancy a sheet of drawing paper.

"Something like this?" he asked.

Nancy's heart gave a leap. On the paper was the sketch of a symbol—the identical crow's-foot F she had seen on Flip Fay's ring!

"That's exactly like it, Lieutenant Hennessy!" she exclaimed.

The officer leaned back in his swivel chair, a smile of satisfaction on his face. "You say you think you saw this man here in Boston?"

Nancy nodded. "Yesterday. Down at the waterfront, near the *Bonny Scot*. He drove away in a taxi, and I tried to follow in mine, but lost him."

"Young lady," the lieutenant said gravely, "you've given us some very important information. This peculiar-looking F is the mark of a dangerous criminal. He's known to the police as The Crow!"

CHAPTER VI

Unexpected Visitors

THE lieutenant said the police had been gathering evidence against The Crow for six months but had not caught up with him.

"We know the jobs that fellow's pulled," the officer said, "because he leaves a crow's footmark behind. Vain fellow, and a clever jewel thief."

"How does he leave it?" Nancy asked.

"Various ways. Cut into wood. Painted on a wall. I guess he was in too much of a hurry to bother with it at your friend's house."

The officer leaned toward Nancy, his voice deliberate. "If I were you, Miss Drew, I would be wary. Extremely wary. The Crow knows you. You interfered with his work once, and he stopped you. If you get in his way again—" Lieutenant Hennessy shook his head gravely.

But Nancy was not thinking of her own safety. She was trying to figure out how Fay might be caught.

"I thought maybe Flip was trying to get away by skipping out of the country," she ventured. "Maybe that's why he's in Boston."

"Perhaps you're right. Thanks to you, Miss Drew, we now know the identity of The Crow. And we have his description. I'll alert all sea-going craft immediately."

Lieutenant Hennessy stood up and shook hands with Nancy. "You've helped us tremendously," he said. "I'll keep in touch with you."

It had been a highly exciting morning, thought Nancy, as she came out of police headquarters. It was now eleven-fifteen and she was to meet the girls at one. Meanwhile, perhaps she could locate the present owner of the *Bonny Scot.* Captain Easterly had said his name was Farnsworth, but had not given his address.

Nancy consulted a telephone directory. There were a number of Farnsworths in the area. She got a supply of coins, and made several telephone calls to the surrounding towns. Finally a Mr. Elijah Farnsworth, real-estate broker, said that he was the owner of the old clipper ship. Identifying herself as Carson Drew's daughter, Nancy made an appointment at his office.

The elderly man received her courteously. "I don't mind saying I'd be proud to do a service for the daughter of a man so highly regarded as your father is by Captain Easterly."

Nancy smiled her appreciation. Then she told

him of the suspicious events that had taken place on board the *Bonny Scot,* and of the damage that had been done to the captain's quarters during his absence.

The owner of the clipper ship bounded from his chair. "Why, that's outrageous!" he declared.

"I'm worried about Captain Easterly," Nancy said. "He hasn't been aboard since day before yesterday. Do you suppose he's being held prisoner somewhere?"

"What's that?" the man asked, astounded.

He declared he would get in touch with the police at once, but Nancy told him this already had been done. She asked Mr. Farnsworth if he had any idea where Captain Easterly might be if he had gone off voluntarily.

"The captain frequently visits his sister in Marblehead. I'll phone her."

The call revealed that the captain had not been to Marblehead for several weeks. Mr. Farnsworth wrinkled his brow, then suddenly snapped his fingers.

"I may have a clue to this mystery after all, Miss Drew," he said. The man drew a slip of paper from his desk drawer and looked at it thoughtfully. "This morning I had a caller. A persistent, determined fellow. He wanted to buy the *Bonny Scot* at once, registration papers or not."

Nancy asked in alarm, "Who was he?"

"His name is Fred Lane. I told him I wouldn't sell to anybody until the title was clear."

"What did he look like, Mr. Farnsworth?" Nancy thought of old Grizzle Face, using an assumed name. "Did he have a gray beard?"

"No, he was clean shaven. Rather tall."

"Did you notice his right hand? Was the middle finger unusually short?"

Mr. Farnsworth looked surprised. "No-o-o, I did notice his fingernails. Clean and well kept."

The caller could not have been Flip Fay. His nails, Nancy remembered, were broken.

"Mr. Lane left his address, in case I should change my mind," Mr. Farnsworth said.

He handed Nancy the slip of paper. Written on it was a number and the name of a street near the Boston waterfront.

Nancy thanked him and put the address into her purse. Excitedly she hurried to the restaurant, where she had agreed to meet Bess and George, and had a snack with them.

Then the three girls taxied to the address Mr. Farnsworth had given Nancy. It proved to be a drab apartment house. Inside the vestibule, they looked for the name "Lane" above the mailboxes. No such name was listed.

Nancy rang the janitor's bell several times. No one answered.

Bess shivered. "Gloomy place. I bet nobody nice lives here."

At that moment a door opened and a shabbily dressed woman came out with a market basket. The door clicked shut after her.

Nancy greeted her courteously. "I beg your pardon, but do you know of a Mr. Lane living at this address?"

The old woman eyed the three girls suspiciously. Then, muttering under her breath, she hurried into the street.

"Did you hear what she said?" asked Nancy.

"It sounded to me like, 'Stay out of here,'" said Bess. "A good idea."

Nancy pressed the janitor's bell once more, but in vain, before deciding to leave. She was a bit discouraged. Her clues had brought no definite results yet.

When she and her friends arrived at the hotel, they were surprised to learn they had visitors. Three young men sitting in the lobby put down their magazines and stood up, grinning.

"Ned Nickerson!" exclaimed Nancy. "How nice to see you!"

"Whatever are you doing here?" asked George. "Lose that job you were going to have at camp?"

The young man laughed. "Can't we relax before going to work? We're here for a weekend of fun."

Dave Evans and Burt Eddleton, college friends of Ned whom the girls knew well, were talking to Bess.

"I hear you've been visiting an old clipper ship," Dave remarked. "And there's a mystery aboard."

"And what a mystery!" exclaimed Bess. "Nancy, you tell them about it."

When Nancy had finished her story, Burt clapped his hand to his head. "And I thought we were just going to do some nice quiet dancing."

"Sounds more exciting to me than dancing," Ned said. "Let's go down to the *Bonny Scot* and look her over."

After the girls had freshened up, they rejoined the young men in the lobby. Then, talking excitedly, the six young people crowded into a large taxicab and directed the driver to take them to the waterfront.

"I wish you didn't want to go back to that ship," Bess told Ned. "It frightens me to death."

Dave laughed. "I'll protect you, Bess—I promise."

"If there are any spooks," said Burt, "they'll have a hard time handling all six of us."

George suggested that they take a short walk along the waterfront "for sea flavor," before boarding the clipper, so they got out two blocks from the ship. Ned walked eagerly ahead with Nancy, while the other two couples—George and Burt, Bess and Dave—lingered behind.

"Let's leave them to their window-shopping," said Nancy. "I want to hurry aboard and see if Captain Easterly has returned."

As the couple stood in front of a cheap water-front restaurant, waiting for the traffic light to change, a man inside caught Nancy's attention. He was sitting at one of the tables, his back to the window.

Nancy touched Ned's arm. "That man!" she whispered excitedly. "He looks like Flip Fay!"

She tried to get a view of the man's profile. "If I could only be sure about him! Ned, do something for me?"

"Anything you say, Nancy."

"Go in there and pretend to be looking for a table. And take a good look at that man's right hand. Find out if it has a short middle finger."

Ned grinned. "Okay, cap'n."

Tensely, Nancy watched Ned swing open the restaurant door, step jauntily inside, and glance toward the table against the window.

Ned was acting his part perfectly. He approached the table where the man with the checkered suit was sitting. Pausing briefly as if looking for an empty table, Ned leaned close to the man Nancy believed was Flip Fay. In his right hand he held a cup of coffee, his middle finger concealed by the cup.

Ned, pretending to trip, deliberately stumbled against the table. The man's cup went down with a bang, half spilling the coffee, and Ned caught a clear glimpse of his short middle finger.

"Sorry," the youth said, regaining his balance.

But the apology was not enough. The person sitting opposite the man rose suddenly, flung back his chair, and took a menacing step toward Ned.

The next instant his right fist shot out and Ned fell backward.

CHAPTER VII

A Suspicious Story

THROUGH the restaurant window Nancy saw Ned fall, then spring to his feet. At the same moment the man in the checkered suit threw back his chair. He and his companion dashed between the tables and through the swinging doors to the kitchen.

"He must have recognized me!" Nancy thought.

She looked wildly up and down the street for a policeman. The nearest one was a traffic officer a block away. She flung open the restaurant door. The few customers looked on astounded at the fracas, while a waitress edged in alarm toward the wall.

"That man in the checkered suit's a dangerous criminal!" Nancy cried. "Stop him!"

She followed Ned through the kitchen doors, just in time to see Flip Fay escape into a side street. His friend was not in sight, Ned said. In a second Fay, too, was swallowed up by the traffic. Nancy and Ned abandoned the chase and returned to the restaurant.

"What was all the racket about?" inquired a fat little man with a toothpick in his mouth. He said he was the owner.

"I think the man in the checkered suit is wanted by the police," Nancy told him. "Do you know who he is?"

The little man shook his head. "No. Nor the guy with him, either."

The waitress who had served the two men spoke up. "They didn't talk like they live around here," the girl said.

"It was Flip Fay, I'm sure," Nancy told Ned. "I must notify the police. It's too bad we didn't get a good look at his friend. Why, Ned, you have a bruise!"

The waitress offered to put a gauze patch on his raw cheekbone. Meanwhile, Nancy stepped into the telephone booth and reported to Lieutenant Hennessy the encounter with Fay. When she finished, Ned was ready to go.

"Let's get down to the ship," he urged. "I'm more curious than ever about the *Bonny Scot*."

They hurried across the dock and boarded the clipper. The other girls were waiting for them with Dave and Burt. They said Captain Easterly had not returned.

"What happened to you, Ned?" Bess asked with concern, looking at his bandaged face.

"One hour with Nancy Drew and I'm in combat," Ned said, grinning.

Nancy told what had happened. Dave and Burt said they were sorry to have missed it. "The three of us could have taken on those two thugs," Dave said ruefully.

"I don't like it," Bess protested. "Somebody's going to get badly hurt if you don't stop interfering with Flip Fay, Nancy."

"The longer a criminal is at large, the more of a menace he is," Ned defended Nancy. "Well, let's look over the *Bonny*."

Burt said he and Dave had pretty well covered everything.

"They don't want to spend their whole weekend snooping over an old ship," Bess declared.

"Let's all meet at the hotel for dinner," George suggested. "And you and Ned be careful, Nancy, do you hear?"

As soon as the others had gone, Nancy showed Ned around the ship. As they descended to the hold of the clipper, she said:

"I've never really had a chance to investigate things down here. I'd like to find out how people get on and off this ship without being seen by the dock guards."

"Black as ink, isn't it?" Ned muttered, directing

the beam of his flashlight over the confusion of barrels and crates and ropes.

"Wait!" Nancy said suddenly. "Put out the light."

Ned obeyed. For a moment the hold seemed utterly dark. Then, as their eyes became accustomed to the dimness, they could see a crack of light near the top of a pile of boxes. The couple made their way toward it and Ned climbed up.

"It's a porthole," he explained. "Not fastened shut," he added, swinging the light around it.

"Look!" Nancy said. "Something's caught in the crack."

Ned picked it up. "A piece of checkered wool," he said excitedly, dropping it to Nancy. "Just like Flip Fay was wearing!"

"You're right, Ned, and he's been through this porthole recently. The cloth is so clean, it couldn't have been here very long."

"So this is how the mysterious visitors have been getting on the ship," Ned mused.

"That's pretty good proof that Flip Fay and Grizzle Face are working together," Nancy replied.

"We'll make sure they don't come through here again," Ned said grimly, starting to fasten the bolts around the rim of the porthole.

"Just a second, Ned," said Nancy. "Will you please look out at that side of the ship under the porthole."

Ned said there were spikes, but that they were hardly noticeable, being painted black like the hull of the *Bonny Scot*. He closed and securely bolted the heavy iron porthole.

He climbed down, and together Nancy and Ned examined every other porthole on the clipper. All were locked.

As they made their way to the captain's cabin, Nancy said she was convinced now that Captain Easterly was being detained somewhere while Grizzle Face and Flip Fay continued their search of the ship for some article of great value. It looked as if a third man, Fred Lane, might be mixed up in the affair.

"Ned, we must find Captain Easterly," Nancy said earnestly. "Something has happened to him—he needs our help!"

"How are we going to find him?" Ned asked. "You've already inquired along the docks, with no luck."

"I haven't given up," Nancy said stoutly. "*Somebody* along the waterfront has certainly seen old Grizzle Face and must know where he lives. Are you game for a bit of sleuthing?"

"Lead the way," Ned ordered, smiling.

Nancy said the only likely places where she and the girls had not inquired were the recreation centers for sailors.

"There's one in particular I'd like you to go into, if you don't mind, Ned," she added.

The youth was quite willing and she led him to an amusement casino. A sign said, TATTOOING DONE CHEAP. Nancy waited outside for several minutes. When Ned came out she could see by his face that he had discovered something.

"The tattoo artist knows your Grizzle Face," he reported. "His name is Red Quint, and here's the address of his boardinghouse."

Nancy was delighted. "Now we're really getting somewhere!" she said enthusiastically.

They found a cab and gave the driver the address.

"You sure you want to go there?" the man asked, turning around to look at them. "It's a tough neighborhood."

Nancy assured him that they wanted to go there, nevertheless. When she saw the house, she understood why the driver had shown some reluctance. It was dingy gray brick with rickety steps leading up to a porch which seemed about to collapse. The shades at the windows were tattered.

"Not exactly homey," Ned remarked, pressing the rusted bell.

They stood there several minutes. There was no sound of approaching footsteps. Then suddenly a window above their heads was flung open.

"What do you want?" a hostile female voice demanded.

Nancy looked up, and met a pair of bleary eyes

in a mottled face. "We're looking for Mr. Red Quint," she said politely.

"Aw, go away." The woman reached up to bang down the window.

"Wait!" Ned pleaded. "We must find Mr. Quint. It's very important."

"He ain't here. He ain't been here for two days." She got the window halfway down.

"May we talk to you a minute longer?" Nancy asked. "Please."

The woman looked doubtful. Finally she stuck out her lower lip and sighed. "Stay there."

She closed the window and presently they could hear her loose slippers flapping down the stairs. She undid a chain on the door and let the callers into a dark hall.

The daylight from outside shone into the woman's eyes and she squinted, trying to get a good look at Nancy and Ned. That moment gave them time to take in the surroundings: the dirty bare floor, the plaster falling from a jagged crack in the wall above a pay telephone. The whole place gave the impression of slovenly housekeeping.

Presently the woman, satisfied that the couple were not bill collectors, rasped out, "Well, what is it you want?"

"Do you know where Red Quint has gone?" Nancy asked.

"How would I know?" the woman grunted. She looked suspiciously at Ned's face bandage.

"Have any friends of Red Quint come here lately?" Nancy went on.

The woman's frowzy gray eyebrows wiggled. "Yeah. Friend of his come here."

"What was his name?"

"I dunno. Seems to me Quint called him Ted or Fred."

Could he have been Fred Lane? Nancy wondered excitedly.

"Is he here?" she asked quickly.

"Naw, he just come and rented a room for his uncle."

"His uncle?" Nancy repeated. "Is he an old man?"

"Middlin'. He's sick. Ain't been out of bed since he come."

Nancy and Ned exchanged excited glances.

"Has he had a doctor?" Nancy inquired, watching the woman carefully.

"Naw. He just don't feel good. Sleeps a lot. They told me to keep an eye on him."

"I must see him," Nancy said, making for the stairs.

"Hey, you can't go up there!" the woman yelled.

But Nancy and Ned were already running up the steps.

CHAPTER VIII

Fire!

NANCY reached the second-floor hallway and knocked on the first door. An angry grunt from inside told her this was not the room.

"Try the front, Ned," she urged. "I'll look in the middle room."

"Nobody in here," Ned reported. "Find anything?"

"No. Let's go up to the next floor."

Nancy bounded up the steps. The woman who had let them in was slowly puffing her way up the first flight of stairs and shouting angrily. Nancy rapped on a door and listened impatiently for sounds within. She heard a groan.

"Ned," she called, "come here!"

Nancy knocked again. There was a murmur inside, and the creak of an old bed.

"There's somebody in there, all right," Ned whispered. He tried the door. It was locked.

"Get away from that room!" screamed the woman, who was halfway up the second flight of stairs. "He's sick, I told you!"

"Can you force the lock?" Nancy asked Ned.

"I'll give it a try." Ned backed away, then came at the door with his shoulder. The lock was old and worn. With one more powerful shove he forced it, and they entered the room.

On an old iron bed lay Captain Easterly. His blue eyes were clouded and dull.

"Captain!" Nancy cried, kneeling beside the bed. "You're ill! How long have you been here?"

He tried to answer her but succeeded only in making an unintelligible murmur.

"We'd better get him out of here right away," Nancy said, turning to Ned. "You stay with him while I go downstairs and call the police."

"What do you think you're doing, young lady?" demanded the woman, who had finally reached the top of the stairs and stood panting in the doorway. "You'd better mind your own business if you know what's healthy for you!"

Nancy said nothing as she hurried down the stairs. She got Lieutenant Hennessy and told him where she was.

"A radio car will be there in three minutes, Miss Drew," he said. "Be careful. You're not among friends."

The police arrived in record time, secured what information they could from the boardinghouse keeper, and transferred Captain Easterly to a hospital. He seemed to improve rapidly, now that he knew he was safe.

He told Nancy, Ned, and the police that while sitting quietly in a waterfront restaurant, sipping a cup of coffee, he had felt very ill. A stranger had offered to help him. They got into a taxi and that was the last thing the captain remembered until Nancy's arrival.

He had been too dizzy to notice what the man looked like. The doctor told them that Easterly's coffee must have been drugged when the captain was not looking. The police set a watch on the boardinghouse to catch the man who had pretended to be the captain's nephew.

It was long past the time Nancy and Ned had agreed to meet the others at the hotel, so after bidding the captain good night, they hurried away. Bess, George, and the boys were already halfway through dinner.

"We couldn't wait any longer," Bess said. "What happened to you two?"

"Plenty." Ned grinned, pulling out a chair for Nancy. "We found Captain Easterly and took him to a hospital."

"What!" George looked amazed, but her eyes fairly popped when they told her where they had found him, and that he had been drugged. "I might have known we'd miss something exciting," she sighed.

Dave turned to Nancy. "If somebody went to all that trouble to get the captain out of the way," he said, "there must be something mighty valuable on the ship."

She nodded. "I wish there were some way to get the clipper out of Boston," she said thoughtfully. "If we could only move it!"

Burt, who was an excellent sailor, reminded her that it was no small trick to sail a clipper ship. "You need some pretty sharp hands aboard."

George put down her fork. "There are six of us. Why couldn't we sail the *Bonny Scot,* with directions from Captain Easterly? We've all practically grown up on sailboats."

"A little pleasure boat is a picnic to sail," Burt spoke up, "compared to a craft like this one. I'll bet, George, you don't even know the names of the masts on the *Bonny Scot.*"

"Yes, I do. Fore, main, and mizzen. And besides, you have the foresail, the staysail, the jibs, the skysails, the—"

"Very salty." Burt grinned. "I apologize."

Nancy said no more about moving the *Bonny Scot,* but she resolved to talk to Captain Easterly about it first thing in the morning. She awoke very early, slipped into her clothes, and left the room without rousing Bess and George. Nancy had a quick breakfast in the hotel coffee shop, and went to the hospital.

Captain Easterly was himself again—his blue

eyes had regained their accustomed glint, and his voice as he greeted her was deep and hearty.

"Get me out of here, Nancy," he begged. "Nothing wrong with me."

Nancy smiled. "We'll see what your doctor says." She sat down and faced him earnestly. "Captain, do you think we could move your ship out of reach of these criminals?" She told him about the boys and their knowledge of sailing gained on the river and the lakes at home.

Captain Easterly looked skeptical. "Pretty big undertaking, Nancy," he said. "But I see your point about getting the clipper out of Boston Harbor. If we could move her at once, before anyone had time to spread the word she was going . . ."

Nancy could see the idea growing in his mind. "I'll send the boys here to talk to you," she offered. "You could give them directions about preparing for the trip. The girls and I could buy the supplies."

The captain's eyes twinkled. "You're a good persuader, Nancy. If we pulled out about dusk, with no fuss and confusion, I'll wager those sneaking rats would be mighty surprised."

The skipper said he would have to notify the Coast Guard, and get a tug to tow them out into the open water. When Nancy left him, he was calling for his clothes and a telephone.

Nancy returned at once to the hotel and found

Ned, Burt, and Dave having breakfast with the girls. She told them that Captain Easterly was willing to sail the clipper to a secluded Cape Cod port. Dave said they would have to work like beavers to make the ship ready.

The three girls set out to purchase food and other supplies for the trip.

When they returned to the hotel, Mr. Drew was waiting for them. After greeting the group, he said to Nancy:

"Captain Easterly is going to be disappointed in my title search. I had no luck in New Bedford. Then I began to suspect that the original name of the clipper was not *Bonny Scot*—but whatever else it might have been, no one I've talked to seems to know. And no measurements matched those of the Bonny Scot."

"You're not giving up, Dad!" Nancy exclaimed.

"You know me better than that." He smiled. "I'm flying down to New York, where, I've been told, there are a great many old records. But what have you been up to, Nancy?"

She told him what had happened to Captain Easterly, and about their plans to move the *Bonny Scot*. She promised to let her father know when they arrived at their destination. Mr. Drew said he would meet them in a few days, and hurried away to catch his plane.

Nancy telephoned Lieutenant Hennessy to ask if he had had any success in tracing Flip Fay,

Grizzle Face Quint, or the man who had drugged Captain Easterly.

"No luck so far," the officer reported. "They've steered clear of that boardinghouse."

The girls packed, and sent their bags separately to the ship, because Nancy thought a lot of luggage arriving at the clipper at the same time might arouse suspicion.

When they reached the dock, the girls found Captain Easterly completely recovered and the boys hard at work. The captain gave Nancy and George the job of sewing up a rip in the main skysail. Bess, who planned to do the cooking, set off to fix up the galley.

To Captain Easterly's delight a heavy fog rolled in at five o'clock. When the tug came alongside, the *Bonny Scot* slipped quietly away from her berth under cover of the mist.

"Wonderful luck!" the captain said to Nancy, who was beside him at the wheel.

A short while later, when they were under full sail, the mist began to lift. Suddenly Nancy thought she saw smoke curling out of a hatch. Not wanting to alarm the captain, she hurried down the companionway, along the passage, and looked into the hold.

The *Bonny Scot* was on fire!

CHAPTER IX

Stowaways

NANCY dashed back to Captain Easterly and told him about the fire. Grimly he signaled for the fireboat, then dropped anchor.

Nancy raced off to give the alarm to the boys. They gathered fire extinguishers and hurried below.

Ned was first into the hold. "If we can keep the fire from spreading, we'll be all right!" he shouted. "Dave, catch it over there near those oil drums!"

Nancy dashed back to the deck to see if a fireboat was coming. Hearing its whistle, she started back to the hold. Nancy got as far as the lowest step of the main companionway when she saw the dark figure of a man disappear around a corner.

"Ned!" Nancy screamed. He did not hear her in the excitement of fighting the fire.

Her heart pounding, she ran after the mysterious, retreating figure. The man ran up a companionway, Nancy not far behind him. When she reached the deck, he had disappeared. As she looked around, Nancy heard a splash.

He had jumped overboard!

She sped across the deck and leaned over the rail. A man was swimming away from the ship's side with long, swift strokes. In the fog Nancy could not see him well enough to identify him.

Reluctantly she had to let the man escape to shore. Unhooking a fire extinguisher on the deckhouse wall, she hurried to the hold. Red-eyed, with wet handkerchiefs tied over their noses, the three boys and George were playing streams of chemical on the smoldering timbers.

Suddenly they heard the churning of water, then shouting voices and heavy-booted footsteps. In a few moments Captain Easterly appeared, followed by a crew of rubber-coated firemen. With their added equipment, the stubborn blaze was soon extinguished.

"Never fought a fire aboard an old clipper before," one of the men told Captain Easterly. "This will be something to tell my grandchildren."

"Your helpers had things pretty well under control when we got here," the fire captain told the ship's master.

"They're a good crew," Easterly admitted.

He and the fireman searched the entire clipper for other signs of fire but found none.

"No serious damage," the fire captain told Easterly. "It'll be safe for you to proceed on your voyage. By the way, how'd the fire start?"

As Captain Easterly shrugged, Nancy spoke up and told about the man who had jumped overboard.

She was very puzzled about him. If he had set the fire on purpose, then he could not be one of the gang looking for a hidden treasure on board. Was he a new enemy?

But if the man had been hiding aboard the *Bonny Scot* when it set sail, in order to continue his search, it was possible he had been smoking and caused the fire accidentally.

"A stowaway, eh?" the fire captain said. "Well, he's gone now. I guess there's nothing more for us to do."

As the firemen were leaving, one of them looked at Nancy and her friends with a twinkle in his eye. "Pretty young crew here, Captain Easterly. But the way they tackled that fire, I'm sure they'll make good seamen."

The men climbed over the side and the fireboat steamed off. The boys pulled up the anchor and set sail.

"Where's Bess?" Nancy asked suddenly. "I haven't seen her since we came aboard."

"I haven't either," said George, beginning to worry about her cousin.

The last they remembered about Bess was that

she was headed for the galley. The two girls hurried there.

Bess was not in sight, but her coat was lying over a low bench. On a hunch Nancy opened the large closet where provisions were kept. Bess lay in a faint on the floor!

Fresh air soon brought her back to consciousness. Groggily Bess explained she had been inside the closet, putting away canned goods, when the door had swung shut.

"I couldn't open it," she said. "It was locked. Then I fainted." Suddenly Bess noticed there was a key in the door. "Why, someone shut me in there!" she cried out.

"It wasn't locked now," Nancy said. "That's odd."

She and George learned that Bess knew nothing about the fire. When it dawned on her that the ship might have been abandoned and she trapped in the fire, Bess nearly fainted again.

"Chin up," George said. "It *didn't* happen. Let's get some food for the boys. I'll bet they're starved after all that work."

"Dave'll like the chocolate cake I brought," said Bess, forgetting her scare. "Why, where is it?" She stared dumfounded at a built-in table in the galley. "The cake's gone!"

"Sure you didn't eat it?" George teased.

"Not even one piece!" Bess declared.

It developed that not only the cake, but a loaf

of bread, a pound of butter, some cooked ham, and two quarts of milk were missing. Both girls looked inquiringly at Nancy, who was deep in thought. Suddenly she said:

"I think we have another stowaway on board!"

Bess and George were astounded at Nancy's statement. Finally George asked:

"How did you figure that one out, Nancy?"

"I think there was someone in the galley stealing food about the time the fire started in the hold. When he heard me call 'Fire!' he unlocked the closet door, Bess, so you wouldn't be caught in a burning ship."

"What about the man who went overboard?" Bess asked.

"I think when I caught him down below deck he had just come up from the hold," Nancy continued. "He may have set the fire either on purpose or accidentally, and was escaping."

George voiced the opinion that the other stowaway must still be on the ship.

"And I mean to find him!" Nancy said.

"Not without me," a voice behind her advised. It was Captain Easterly. "While George and Bess get supper, you and I will make a thorough search, Nancy."

They went about the hunt methodically, first in the cabins and crew's quarters, then in the hold, and finally in the old sea chests and cupboards. There was no sign of a stowaway or of the food that had vanished.

"Our thief must have been the fellow who jumped overboard," the captain concluded.

Nancy was not satisfied with this explanation. He certainly had no food with him when he dived in. Aloud she said:

"I wonder if the fellow who jumped overboard got to shore safely."

"Likely he helped himself to a ride on the fireboat," Captain Easterly suggested.

"Of course!"

Nancy berated herself for not having thought of this. The man might have been caught! Now it was too late, because the fireboat would have long since docked.

Captain Easterly suddenly chuckled. "That snooper thought he was going to find out where we're heading. But we fooled him. Now we can sail and enjoy ourselves. No more worries."

Nancy wished she could agree with him—especially since they had outridden the fog bank, and the cool evening with its freshening breeze was ideal for the voyage.

"But we must be watchful," Nancy determined.

The boys took turns eating supper. While Ned was off watch, Nancy asked him to do a little further exploring with her.

The young detective had decided to take one

more look in the hold where the fire had been. The person who caused the fire might have left a clue.

Descending the narrow wooden steps, she walked carefully through the dark space, swinging her flashlight here and there. The heavy smell of smoke and wet timber still hung in the air. Reaching the spot where the fire had been, Nancy leaned over to examine the charred timbers.

"Ned, see what's here!" she called excitedly.

Near the burned area was a deep, newly cut hole in the wall. It had not been there when she and Captain Easterly were searching half an hour before!

CHAPTER X

An Unusual Box

ABOUT three feet from the charred flooring, beneath the newly made hole, lay a hatchet. Nancy and Ned had the same thought. They had surprised someone at work! The stowaway had felt safe to search while the ship's passengers were busy elsewhere.

"Where can he be?" Ned asked, looking behind the piles of boxes and crates.

Nancy examined every inch of the old walls, which were full of markings of a bygone day. She hoped that among them might appear the outline of a secret door. She found none. Ned was no more successful.

"Your guess about two stowaways was right, Nancy," he said as he gave up the search. "And one of them is still aboard."

It was maddening—and ridiculous—that he and

Nancy could not catch him, Ned added. The stowaway seemed to be able to come and go as easily as a ghost.

"We must tell Captain Easterly at once," Nancy said.

They went directly to his cabin, but he was not there. Nancy, seeing a small object on the floor near the captain's desk, bent over and picked it up.

"An old snuffbox," she said. "Isn't it pretty?"

On the lid was a cameo—the face of a lovely woman. She had long curling hair and a serene expression.

"Ned, this may be just what I've been looking for!" Nancy exclaimed suddenly.

"What do you mean?"

"This woman on the box is probably the copy of a figurehead on a ship. She may be the one from the *Bonny Scot!*"

Ned smiled. "Aren't you jumping to conclusions?"

Nancy dashed up to the quarterdeck where Captain Easterly was scanning the overcast sky.

"Where did you get this snuffbox?" she asked him excitedly, holding it under a light.

The captain looked at the article on the girl's outstretched hand. "I never saw it before," he answered.

"Then the stowaway dropped it," Nancy told him, and brought the skipper up to date on the

"Ned, this may be what I've been looking for!"

finding of the hole and the hatchet, proving that some mysterious intruder was still aboard.

Captain Easterly frowned. "But where in thunder can he be?"

Nancy's eyes lighted up. "I think I know how we might catch him."

"How?"

"He's raided the galley once, and I have a hunch he'll come back for drinking water. Ned, let's set a watch for him!"

Ned's eyes sparkled. "You really keep trying—that's what I like about you, Nancy."

Captain Easterly smiled tolerantly. "You're such a good sleuth, Nancy, I might as well say Yes to your scheme. Ned and Dave can watch."

He glanced at the sky and frowned. "We may be in for a squall. I'm going to shorten sail."

The captain put the boys to work. Nancy joined the girls. She told them the plan to surprise the stowaway in the ship's galley that night. One of the boys would wait inside the galley door. The other boy would rest in a small cabin directly across the passageway.

"And now I have something to show you," Nancy said.

She held out the snuffbox. "I think our stowaway must have dropped this. Perhaps he found it during one of his hatchet parties."

"Or he may have brought it aboard with him," suggested George.

Studying the box more closely, Nancy discovered the initials P. R. and the date 1850.

"I'm sure we've hit upon a clue," she remarked to the girls. "Captain Easterly said this clipper might have been built about that time. And Dad thought the original name might have been changed to *Bonny Scot.*"

"You mean P. R. might be this clipper's initials?" Bess asked.

"Maybe. Let's see what we can find in the captain's book."

They went to his cabin and found the book which listed famous clipper ships. They read the names together: *Rainbow, Flying Cloud, Sovereign of the Seas, Red Jacket, Lightning.*

"What romantic names they gave those old clippers," Bess sighed. "But none of them has the initials P. R."

Nancy frowned thoughtfully. "As soon as I'm ashore again, I'm going to do some research."

George had taken off the lid and was smelling the inside of the box. "It's a snuffbox if you say so. But it's never had any snuff in it."

"Maybe there was something valuable inside— a note of some sort," Bess suggested. She yawned. "I'm dreadfully sleepy, girls. Why don't we go to our bunks? Stowaway or not, I've got to get some sleep. I'll lock my door."

George grinned. "After you're sure no one's under the bunk."

Through the night Ned and Dave took turns watching. By four o'clock no one had come near the galley. Nancy had dropped into an uneasy sleep when she was awakened by the sound of running feet and distant shouting.

Nancy threw on a coat and dashed from her cabin. In the darkness she ran full tilt into someone.

"Ned!" she gasped. "Are you all right?"

"I'm okay," he told her. "No stowaway, Nancy. I heard the captain calling. Let's get up on deck and see what's wrong."

As she ran up the companionway Nancy could feel the ship heaving and tossing. On deck they found the captain shouting orders to Dave, who was going aloft to struggle with a whipping sail on the mainmast. Burt was at the wheel.

"Got to shorten more sail," Captain Easterly bellowed. "Going to be a blow. We tried to run for it, but we're caught. All we can do now is make things fast and ride her out. Nancy, you and Ned take the wheel and relieve Burt. I need him."

The wind increased. The waves rose and crashed over the deck. It was all the couple could do to hold the ship on the course the captain had set. The rain pelted down in the inky darkness.

Clinging to the wheel, Nancy looked around her in fascinated horror. Waves broke over the forecastle head and raced along the deck. Above her the rigging hummed and jangled.

Captain Easterly fought his way back to the drenched girl and grasped the wheel.

"Get below, Nancy!" he bellowed.

Grasping the rigging and the rail, Nancy finally reached the companionway and half slid, half fell to the passageway below.

She found Bess and George in the captain's cabin. Bess was lying on the bunk, hanging onto the side with both hands. George, who had gone to help but had been sent back, was sitting on top of the built-in desk, clutching the porthole frame.

Furniture that was not bolted down was sliding from one end of the cabin to the other. Nancy fell into the bunk with Bess.

"The storm's bound to blow itself out pretty soon," Nancy said, trying to be cheerful. "I wonder how the stowaway's making out."

"It would serve him right if he got all banged up," George said bitterly.

Within a few minutes the deafening roar of the wind slackened suddenly. The noise of the crashing waves was not so terrifying.

Nancy decided to go back to the wheel. Maybe she could be helpful. What a different scene from the one a short time before! The storm was over. In the distance twinkling lights on shore mingled with streaks of gray in the early-morning sky.

"We're making for a cove," Ned told her.

Bess and George had come up on deck, and

everyone watched as Captain Easterly dropped anchor in the deep water of the cove.

Then the captain ordered a hearty breakfast for his weary workers. Nancy and George quickly set the long table in the galley, while Bess fried enormous quantities of bacon and eggs. After they had been consumed, the skipper suggested sleep for his guests. Exhausted, they obeyed, while he remained on watch.

By ten o'clock Nancy and her friends were up and around again. Captain Easterly thanked them for their good sportsmanship.

"You're real mariners," he said.

"And the *Bonny Scot*'s a swell ship," Dave spoke up. "I hope you get a clear title, so you can buy her, Captain Easterly. And I hope you invite us to take a sail with you."

"So do I," said Burt.

"Don't forget me." Ned laughed.

The captain's eyes twinkled. "Want me to ask the girls, too?"

"Why not?" said Ned. "Every clipper needs cooks."

The girls grimaced, then Ned said, "I hate to change the subject, but we fellows will have to get to camp or lose our jobs, Captain. Will you and the girls be safe here in the cove if we leave?"

Captain Easterly nodded. "Safe as a clam in a shell. We'll even catch our stowaway, unless he's swum to land already."

Since the dinghy carried only four passengers, it was decided that Nancy would go ashore with the boys and row the boat back.

"Now you can get some sleep, Captain Easterly," Bess said kindly.

Nancy was glad of the opportunity to notify her father that the ship was safe in the cove, and to do a little exploring in the nearby waterfront town. She had the unusual-looking snuffbox in her purse as she climbed into the boat.

"Be careful," Bess called after her, leaning anxiously over the side. "Grizzle Face or Flip Fay may be around!"

"I'll watch out," Nancy promised.

The boys caught a bus for Boston and Nancy was left alone on the main street of the little town. She found that telegrams could be sent from the grocery-hardware store.

Nancy wired Mr. Drew at his sister's apartment in New York City. Then she said to the proprietor, "Is there anyone in town who knows about the history of clipper ships?"

"Clippers?" The man scratched his head and thought a moment. "Used to be a number of old-timers here who could have told you some tall tales, miss. I reckon the only fellow who takes an interest in such things now is Walt Frisbie."

"Where does he live?"

"At the end of this street. He's got a shop in an old barn where he carves out figureheads."

Nancy was excited. Figureheads! She thanked him, then hurried along Main Street until she came to a sign on a post:

WALTER FRISBIE
FIGUREHEADS

"This is just too good to be true," Nancy thought excitedly.

She followed a sandy path to the open barn door, stepped inside, and found herself in a fascinating room. A few restored figureheads leaned against the walls, but most of Mr. Frisbie's possessions were figures without heads, or heads without bodies.

At a worktable, on which lay an enormous block of black wood, stood a tall, middle-aged man with bushy black eyebrows. Mr. Frisbie had a chisel in his hand, and he looked as if he would like to use it on Nancy for disturbing him.

"I'm busy," he said shortly. "What do you want?"

Nancy smiled. "I'm very sorry to interrupt you, Mr. Frisbie, but I've been told you're the only man around here who takes an interest in old clipper ships. I need your help."

His frosty face softened. "What are you up to, young lady?"

Nancy took the snuffbox from her purse and held it out to him. "Have you ever seen a figurehead like this cameo?"

Mr. Frisbie studied it with great interest. "Where did you get this?"

"On a ship called the *Bonny Scot.*"

Nancy told him briefly about the lost figurehead of the clipper and how eager Captain Easterly was to find out what it had looked like.

Mr. Frisbie put down his chisel and examined the little box. He could not recall having seen that particular figurehead, he said, nor did he know of any clipper whose initials were P. R.

"My father has been trying to get a clear title to the *Bonny Scot,*" Nancy explained, "but so far he hasn't found any record of her at all. We wondered if the ship's name might have been changed."

"Tell you what," the woodcarver suggested. "I have quite a library of books on clippers and old sailing ships upstairs. Why don't you browse around?"

"Oh, may I? That would be wonderful!"

Mr. Frisbie pointed out a narrow stairway leading to the loft of the barn.

Nancy thanked him and climbed to the loft. She was delighted to find an unusual collection of rare volumes and drawings, and sat down on an old grain box to look through them. She began by comparing the cameo with the illustrations of figureheads.

The sun climbed high. Nancy was lost in the fascinating tales of another day.

Mr. Frisbie poked his head up into the loft. "Don't you ever eat, girl?" he demanded.

"I hadn't thought about it," Nancy confessed. "But I *am* hungry." She took time to hurry into town for a sandwich and a glass of milk, then returned to Mr. Frisbie's studio.

At half past five he came up and stood beside her. "Sorry," he said, "but I lock up about this time. Glad to have you come back tomorrow, if you want to."

"I do want to, very much," Nancy told him. "I haven't found my figurehead."

"You stick to it like a bulldog, don't you?" Mr. Frisbie laughed. "You'd make a good detective."

Nancy smiled, dropped the snuffbox into her purse, and hurried along the main street toward the waterfront, and the beach where she had left the dinghy.

Suddenly hearing stealthy footsteps behind her, Nancy whirled.

There stood Grizzle Face!

He snatched her bag. Nancy clutched at it, but quick as a wink the man emptied its contents.

He seized the snuffbox triumphantly.

CHAPTER XI

A Favorite Lady

NANCY caught his arm and tried to take the little box from him. But Grizzle Face, muscular and wiry, shook her off easily and dashed away.

"You can't have that!" Nancy cried, running after him.

"It's mine!" he flung over his shoulder.

She tried desperately to catch up to him. Her mind raced with only one thought: she *had* to question him.

"I know you were a stowaway on the *Bonny Scot!*" Nancy called after him. "Please! I only want to question you."

But Grizzle Face kept on running. If only someone would come to help her capture him!

"The police will get you!" she called, hoping to scare him.

The word *police* worked like magic. Grizzle Face halted in his tracks. "Police?" he said. "I ain't a thief."

"You can keep the snuffbox," Nancy said, stopping. "Just answer a few questions for me."

"Don't come any closer," Grizzle Face ordered, "and maybe I'll talk." Nancy did not move. "Yeah, I was on the clipper. That satisfy you?"

"Where were you during the storm?" Nancy asked. "We looked everywhere for a stowaway."

The sailor seemed gratified. "I know that ship better'n old Easterly does. There's places."

"What sort of places?" Nancy insisted.

"Never mind."

"You've sailed on her before?" There was no answer to that, so Nancy continued, "The snuffbox has some connection with the *Bonny Scot*, hasn't it? The cameo is like the figurehead that used to be on it."

Involuntarily the man opened his big hand and glanced at the snuffbox. "Where'd you get that idea?" he grunted.

Nancy felt that she was getting somewhere. If she could take him off guard, perhaps he would say something revealing.

"You stole the box!" she accused him suddenly.

"I did not! It belongs to me!"

"Is that so?" Nancy looked at him skeptically. "You stole it from Captain Easterly's cabin."

"You think you know a lot, don't you? Well, maybe you can tell me how the mate happened to have it, then."

"The mate?" Nancy repeated eagerly.

Red Quint gave her a startled look, as if just realizing he had said something wrong. With three long strides he was at the top of the nearest sand dune and down the other side.

Nancy ran after him, tripped as her heel caught the top of a hummock, and fell. By the time she struggled to her feet and reached the top of the dune, Quint had vanished.

The little mounds of sand, tufted with stiff grass, stretched for miles along the shore. He probably had dropped flat behind one of them and was waiting for her to go away.

Quint was an unsavory character, Nancy knew. She decided it would be wiser for her to return to the clipper than to hunt for him.

"But I ought to notify the police," she told herself. "After all, Quint was mixed up with the captain's kidnapper."

Nancy retrieved her handbag and then retraced her steps to town and found the local state trooper's office. He promised to start a search for Quint at once and to alert headquarters.

"I hope he won't shave off his grizzly beard, so he can't be identified," Nancy reflected as she hurried back to the beach.

She shoved the dinghy into the water, and jumped into the boat. As Nancy bent to the oars, she reflected on the strange information Red Quint had given her. Where had he managed to hide on the ship so that even the captain could not find him? What had he meant when he said the mate had the snuffbox? The mate of the *Bonny Scot* in the old days? She wondered if Red ever had sailed on the clipper.

She was still some distance from the ship when Bess shouted, "Here she comes!"

The girls put down the ladder and helped Nancy aboard, scolding her and asking dozens of questions.

"We thought you'd been drowned, kidnapped, or cut in small pieces!" George told her. "Where were you?"

Nancy told them and Captain Easterly of her visit to Mr. Frisbie and of the struggle with Grizzle Face.

"I'm sure he's the one who dropped the snuffbox in your cabin, Captain Easterly," she concluded. "He says he got it from 'the mate.' What mate do you suppose he means?"

The captain said he had no idea.

"Quint said there are hiding places on the clipper that even you don't know about," Nancy went on.

"That's possible," Captain Easterly admitted reluctantly. "Especially if the ship was ever used by pirates. They were a devilish, clever lot. But look here, it's high time to eat."

Nancy and the girls followed him down to the galley where they ate the delicious supper Bess had prepared.

Next morning George and Bess said they wanted to go along with Nancy to Mr. Frisbie's shop. They left Captain Easterly to guard the clipper and enjoy the cool breeze under the deck awning.

The three girls rowed to shore. The first thing Nancy did was call State Police headquarters and ask if Red Quint had been found. There was no word about the man.

When they arrived at the barn, Mr. Frisbie greeted them with a smile. "I see you brought reinforcements," he said.

"Yes," said Nancy, and introduced her friends. "We'd like to see your interesting old books and drawings again, if you don't mind."

"Go ahead. Glad to find somebody that enjoys them," he said.

All morning the girls pored over the volumes whose pages were yellow with age.

Later the three friends dined in a little garden tearoom, and afterward walked along a winding road to a cluster of weathered gray cottages. They were occupied by artists who came to paint the sea and the quaint village. The girls watched some of them at work.

Then, at Nancy's suggestion, Bess and George returned to the ship, donned their swimsuits, and spent a delightful afternoon in the water and on the beach.

While they were swimming, Nancy again

searched for a clue in Mr. Frisbie's old books. She read for some time, but came upon no information on ships with names whose initials could be P. R.

At five o'clock the girls picked her up and rowed back to the *Bonny Scot*. After supper they came up on deck and dropped into comfortable chairs.

The captain leaned back and lit his pipe as the girls discussed the missing figurehead. "More than one ship has lost its figurehead, for one reason or another," he said.

"Did they ever change the figurehead on purpose?" George wanted to know.

Captain Easterly puffed on his pipe. "Sometimes they did. For instance, if a ship had a new captain, maybe he wouldn't like the figurehead. So he'd change it for one he picked out himself."

Nancy was thinking about another figurehead —the lovely woman carved on the snuffbox she had found.

"I wish I knew more about the mystery of that snuffbox," she said. "It must be valuable if old Grizzle Face wanted it. I'll keep on looking till I find the history of it. I have a hunch that figurehead was on this ship."

"Can you still remember what it looked like?" Bess asked.

"I can now, but I'm afraid I'll forget later,"

Nancy admitted. "I'll make a sketch of it first thing in the morning."

"I'm glad you said 'morning,'" George confessed. "I can hardly keep my eyes open."

The girls said good night to the captain and went below.

Captain Easterly stayed on deck and slept fitfully. Nothing happened, and morning dawned peacefully.

After breakfast Captain Easterly handed Nancy a box of pencils, crayons, and drawing paper he had on board. She set to work sketching the cameo from the snuffbox as best she could from memory. Nancy was so busy that she did not hear an approaching rowboat.

"Ahoy, there!" called a man's voice.

"Dad!" Nancy jumped to her feet.

He came aboard, smiling. "Looks like an industrious and peaceful crew you've got here, Captain Easterly."

The skipper shook hands with him. "At the moment, Yes. But we've had our troubles."

"What's this?" Mr. Drew turned to his daughter. "More excitement aboard the *Bonny Scot?*"

"Mr. Drew, you should have been here during the storm!" Bess exclaimed. "It was simply horrible."

"It was exciting," George and Nancy said together, laughing.

The girls told him about the voyage from Boston, the fire, the storm, and the two stowaways, one of whom had jumped overboard.

Mr. Drew frowned. "You're lucky to be alive."

"The other stowaway was Red Quint. He was aboard all the time," George reported.

"He was looking for something," Nancy explained. "But we have no idea what. He dropped a snuffbox with a cameo of a lady on it—like this." She showed her father the half-finished sketch.

"Handsome woman," Carson Drew commented. "Why are you sketching her?"

"Because I think she was a figurehead," Nancy replied. "I have a hunch she was the figurehead on the *Bonny Scot!*"

The lawyer became more interested. "I see you've made some progress on the case."

"That she has," said the captain.

"I still have a long way to go before solving the mystery."

Her father looked at her intently. Then he turned to the skipper of the *Bonny Scot*. "Captain Easterly," he said, "I'm afraid I have bad news for you."

CHAPTER XII

A Pirate's Prize

"DAD," Nancy said in alarm, "what has happened?"

"Oh, nothing to frighten anyone," the lawyer replied. "Just a big disappointment. I have absolutely nothing to report about the title to this ship. I studied every record I could get hold of. Visited shipbuilding companies and libraries, even talked to old seamen. There isn't a single mention of a clipper named the *Bonny Scot,* and nobody's ever heard of her."

"And no clue to any other name?" Nancy asked.

Mr. Drew shook his head. "Of course," he admitted, "there are no records for many of the old ships. It hurts my pride to render a negative report, Captain, especially now that I must give up the case."

"What do you mean, Dad?" Nancy asked.

"I've been called back to River Heights," her

ST. JOHN THE BAPTIST PARISH LIBRARY
2920 NEW HIGHWAY 51
LAPLACE, LOUISIANA 70068

father said. "A case coming up in court. I must leave here this afternoon. Terribly sorry, Captain."

Mr. Drew looked at his daughter. There was a challenge in his eye. "But how about you staying? If you use the ingenuity and the perseverance I credit you with, Nancy, I believe you'll solve the case. What do you say?"

Nancy hugged her father, then laughed. "You know, for a minute I thought you were going to make me go home with you. Of course I'll stay, if Captain Easterly will let me."

The skipper grunted. "Don't you girls dare leave me alone with this mystery!"

He said he had a feeling that by solving the mystery of why the intruders came on the ship, the matter of title would be cleared up too.

"And I think Nancy's the one who can do it," the captain said staunchly.

After lunch Nancy told her friends she would row her father over to the village, to take his bus for the airport. "I think while I'm in town, I'll stop at Mr. Frisbie's."

"Again?" George teased. "Count me out this time."

"If you don't mind," said Bess, "I'll stay here and write a letter home, then go for a swim." George decided to stay with her cousin.

Nancy wanted her friends to have some vacation fun at Cape Cod, and said that there was no need for them to accompany her.

Before going to the barn, Nancy once more called the State Police. There was no report on Grizzle Face Quint.

Mr. Frisbie did not seem surprised when Nancy walked into the studio. He said, "Good afternoon!" with his usual abruptness, but his frosty blue eyes softened in a smile as he waited for her to climb the steps to the second floor. Instead, Nancy stood still, staring at what had once been a large block of black wood on the workbench. Now it had the rough outline of a small body.

"Is this going to be a figurehead?" Nancy asked.

"Yes, and by the time she's finished, the young lady will weigh only twenty pounds," Mr. Frisbie said. "She started out at four hundred." He grinned.

"You mean you have to throw away all that wood?" Nancy thought this was a dreadful waste.

"Nowadays, figureheads are carved from a solid block, and usually from ebony, like this one," Mr. Frisbie explained. "Then no heads or legs can drop off like in the old days when the parts were jointed together."

The sculptor said even hard woods like oak were not as durable as ebony, and in his work he would use nothing but the best. "After all, I'm creating a beautiful young lady," he said.

Nancy chuckled as she left to go upstairs. Presently she was deep again in the study of Mr. Frisbie's books on sailing ships.

Suddenly a new thought struck her. Perhaps the initials P. R. stood for a person instead of a ship! If the design carved on the snuffbox were a ship's figurehead, couldn't the P. R. refer to the ship's master?

Eagerly the young detective began looking for the names of captains whose initials were P. R. She would pay special attention to ships whose fates were unknown.

This new lead had some exciting results. She learned from one of the books, which looked as if it had been through many a hurricane, about a vessel named the *Dream of Melissa*.

The clipper was on her way home to Provincetown from Bombay, under the command of Captain Perry Rogers. When last seen she had been heading for Sunda Strait, between Java and Sumatra.

No one knew what had happened to the *Dream of Melissa*. She had simply disappeared. So far as was known, no trace of the ship or cargo had ever been found. Neither captain nor crew had ever been heard from again!

Nancy's eyes were bright with excitement. The *Melissa's* captain, Perry Rogers, had the initials P. R. The snuffbox could have been his! The figure on it was a dreamy-faced woman. She might well be the Melissa of the ship's name!

The *Dream of Melissa* had carried a costly cargo of rugs, silks, and perfumes.

"Surely a pirate's prize!" Nancy reflected.

Captain Easterly had told her that the clippers sailing to and from the Far East had often been attacked by pirates. He had even mentioned that the islands off Java were a favorite hideout for these sea gangsters.

Perhaps, Nancy thought excitedly, pirates had seized the *Dream of Melissa*. If they intended to keep the ship, of course they would have to change her name. And naturally they would get rid of the figurehead—it was too good a clue to the ship's identity.

Nancy closed the book. "The *Bonny Scot*," she told herself, "may really be the *Dream of Melissa*."

Her eyes aglow, she ran to the first floor to speak to Mr. Frisbie. All she found was a crisp note:

Lock up when you leave.

Smiling, Nancy looked at her watch. Six o'clock! She locked the barn door, hurried to the dinghy, and made fast time out to the clipper. Her eager face told the others she had found something this time.

"Out with it," George demanded.

After Nancy had told her story, Bess shivered. "My goodness, to think I may have been sleeping in some pirate's bunk!"

"Those stowaways may know about the pirates and think there's hidden loot on board!" George added.

"Now just a minute, girls," Captain Easterly spoke up. "Seems to me you're jumping to conclusions. In the morning we'll make plans for tracking down this dream ship of yours, Nancy," he said. "No more work tonight."

But Nancy could not get the *Dream of Melissa* out of her mind. She lay awake, wondering if the *Bonny Scot* could have borne that other name. If it had been captured by pirates, what had happened to Captain Perry Rogers? Was it to his mate Grizzle Face had referred?

Such exciting thoughts kept Nancy wide awake until after midnight. Captain Easterly, she knew, had been too tired to remain on watch and had gone to his cabin. George and Bess were sleeping peacefully in their bunks. Nancy heard nothing but the soft slap of water on the ship's side and the creaking of the masts.

Suddenly a new sound made her sit straight up, nerves tingling. Just outside her porthole she heard a soft *thump, thump, thump!*

Nancy slid out of her bunk and threw on a coat. Slipping a flashlight from under her pillow, she tiptoed into the passageway and knocked on the captain's door.

"Captain Easterly, there's someone on board!" she called softly.

Then, without waiting for him to appear, she ran up to the deck.

CHAPTER XIII

The Shadowy Figure

NANCY stopped at the top of the companionway. She could see nothing clearly. If someone had come aboard he might be crouching close to her on the shadowy deck. She moved forward cautiously.

Heavy mist swirled about the ship, making the masts and rigging seem vague and unreal. Somewhere in the distance a foghorn wailed.

Suddenly Nancy froze, her hands clenched. A figure was coming over the rail, directly in front of her! Nancy slipped quickly into the shadows. Whoever he was, he had not seen her. She had the advantage!

The intruder dropped catlike to the deck, then moved quickly out of sight in the mist. Nancy made her way cautiously after him. If only she could see the stranger's face!

Would he turn around if she flashed her light on him?

"I'll try it," she decided, and snapped on the light.

The man was startled but did not turn around. Bent almost double, with his sleeve raised to conceal the side of his face, he scurried ahead into the shrouding mist.

Nancy ran after him, but he disappeared in the inky shadows. She had not heard a splash. He must still be aboard!

Nancy's heart beat rapidly. It was one thing for her to follow a fugitive she could see, but quite another to have a stranger jump at her from some dark spot.

Where was Captain Easterly? Nancy thought uneasily as she pondered what to do next. To her relief, the skipper's voice boomed out behind her.

"Nancy, where are you? What's up?"

Quickly Nancy retraced her steps and in whispered tones told him what had happened. "I'm sure the man's still aboard," she concluded. "Maybe he's gone below."

"We'll look up here first," the captain ordered.

Swinging their flashlights, he and Nancy covered the damp planking, the coiled ropes and hawsers, the rigging, the hatch covers. There was no sign of the man they were hunting. Before going below to continue the search, Captain Easterly said:

"Where did he come aboard?"

Nancy led the skipper to the spot where she had seen the intruder come over the side. As they reached it, their flashlights revealed a rope wriggling over the rail. A moment later it dropped to the water. Together they bent over the rail, sweeping the water with their flashlights. A man was sitting in a rowboat!

"Who are you? Stop!" the captain roared.

The fugitive did not answer. He hunched his head into his shoulders, shoved an oar against the *Bonny Scot,* and the rowboat slid away into the billowing mist.

"Oh, dear," Nancy sighed. "I didn't get a good look at him. Did you, Captain?"

"No, but he's probably a desperate character, Nancy. You were mighty foolish to come up here without me."

"I know," Nancy said contritely, "but I was afraid we'd lose him."

In the dim light Nancy could see the captain's face break into a broad smile. He took her arm. "Now that I've scolded you, I want to thank you for driving him off the ship. Better get below and finish your night's sleep," he added.

"Wait, Captain Easterly!" Nancy begged. "That man may have dropped something that will identify him. By morning it might be gone."

"You're right. I wouldn't have thought of such a thing," the skipper said.

"Stop!" the captain roared

Already Nancy was hurrying toward the spot where the intruder had come aboard. She beamed her flashlight around the planking all the way to the rail. A moment later she stooped down, picked something up, and cried out:

"He did leave a clue! Captain Easterly, it's a good one! He dropped a book of matches!"

The skipper came running up. "A book of matches?"

Nancy grabbed his arm. "Captain, look! It's an ad for the Owl Restaurant in River Heights!"

"You mean where you live?" the captain asked, astounded.

"Yes. And that means—"

Nancy paused a moment as more evidence presented itself. Upon opening the matchbook, she had seen something scribbled in pencil.

"What does it say?" the captain demanded, looking over her shoulder. "My eyes aren't that good."

"M-a-r-v-i-n." Nancy spelled out the crudely printed name, which was followed by Bess's address. Without doubt the matchbook belonged to the man who had stolen the Marvin jewelry. The person whom they had chased off the clipper was Fay, The Crow! Captain Easterly had been correct in his hunch. Their caller *was* a desperate character!

It took Captain Easterly a few minutes to follow Nancy's reasoning. When he did, he became very much concerned.

"What was this unsavory character doing on my ship?" he stormed. "I don't understand."

Nancy agreed it was puzzling. "I'm sure now that Flip Fay and Red Quint are working together. Grizzle Face notified him where we are."

"But what are they working at, that's what I want to know." The captain pounded the rail. "What is on this ship that robbers and kidnappers go creeping through her like a lot of devilish ghosts!"

Nancy gave him a puzzled smile. "I don't know, Captain, but I'm going to find out what it is and where it is before somebody steals it!"

"Fine, fine," he agreed. "But let's not worry any more about it tonight," he added, calming down. "That crook won't be back in a hurry. He knows we're waiting for him. Go to bed, Nancy, and be sure to lock your cabin door. We'll have a conference over the breakfast pancakes."

Nancy went below and slid quietly into her bunk without waking the other girls. She lay there a long time thinking about the many baffling things that had happened on the *Bonny Scot* since the first day when she and her father had come aboard to meet Captain Easterly.

She wondered whether Flip Fay and Grizzle Face had known each other before Fay came to

Boston. Perhaps they had been to sea together and had learned something that had led them to the clipper. Could it be that Fay was the "mate" that Grizzle Face had referred to on the dunes? And what about the man who had drugged and kidnapped the captain—was he Fred Lane? What had become of him?

Nancy always came back to the original question—what was the true name of the *Bonny Scot?* It seemed impossible to get anywhere with the puzzle until they knew that. Undoubtedly Quint, Fay, and Lane called the ship something else.

They had heard some tale about the clipper's past which had led them to believe a treasure was concealed on it. What was the treasure? Something very small, Nancy decided, or it would have been found long ago. Something small and priceless, something . . .

Nancy awakened to the delicious odor of frying bacon, floating in from the galley. The bunks were empty. It must be late, she thought, jumping up.

Nancy quickly dressed and joined the captain and the girls, who were already at breakfast in the officer's quarters. Bess and George were talkative, but Captain Easterly was silently thoughtful. He set down his cup of coffee onto the saucer with a little click of finality.

"Girls," he announced with effort, "you can't

stay here any longer. None of you must remain
another day on the *Bonny Scot!*"

"What!" The three girls stared at him in
amazement.

"It isn't safe. Flip Fay was on board last night."
The skipper frowned. "And Nancy was up on
deck chasing him."

"Nancy, you weren't?" Bess shuddered.

"Hypers! Why didn't you call me?" George demanded.

Nancy said she would have, if she had guessed
what was going to happen. She told them about
the matchbook, and about her thoughts of the
night before.

"We *must* find out if the original name of this
clipper was the *Dream of Melissa*," she said earnestly. "Captain Easterly, wouldn't a ship's name
be marked on furniture and things?"

He gave her a shrewd smile. "You're trying to
distract me. The question before the council is,
When do you girls leave?"

Bess protested vigorously, "We're not going,
Captain. We can't leave you here all alone with
these vicious characters sneaking around."

"That goes for me, too," George said stoutly.

"So you see, Captain," Nancy concluded, "you
may as well forget about dropping your crew over
the side and take up the matter of the true name
of the *Bonny Scot*."

Captain Easterly rubbed his face with a big red hand and looked from one to the other. "I surrender. You may stay, but I'm going to arrange for a guard to watch this ship tonight. Now about the name being on furniture—how long do you think seagoing furniture lasts? The clipper's been scudding around this world a good many years, and I would guess that most of her original fittings have been replaced."

"Perhaps something remains," said Nancy.

George rose to make more pancakes and went into the galley. She was gone an unusually long time.

"George, what's keeping you?" Bess called.

A moment later her cousin cried out excitedly, "Come here, everybody! I've found it!"

CHAPTER XIV

A Strange Warning

NANCY and Bess dashed into the galley, followed by Captain Easterly.

George was on her hands and knees, her head under a crude wooden bench nailed to the floor. In her hand was a spoon which had fallen under the bench.

"Poke your head down here and look at this!" she exclaimed.

Nancy dropped to the floor. On the underside of the bench she saw carved letters that made her gasp.

"Captain," she cried, "it says Dr. of Mel. The *Bonny Scot* is the *Dream of Melissa!*"

"What? Let me see!" Captain Easterly got down on his knees. "You're right!"

"The snuffbox fits in, too," Nancy reasoned, "because the master of the *Dream of Melissa* was Captain Perry Rogers."

"And the carving on the snuffbox must be a copy of the figurehead of Captain Rogers' ship!" George exulted.

Bess sighed thoughtfully. "That woman looked like somebody sweet and dreamy who might be named Melissa."

Nancy was too excited to eat any more breakfast. She said the next thing to do was look for further clues to check the carving in the galley.

"We'll investigate every piece of furniture on the ship," she told Captain Easterly.

"Let's begin here," George suggested, turning a chair upside down.

They went over the ship's furniture carefully but found no lettering. Then they took the cabins, one by one. George climbed into the upper bunks and looked at the woodwork, and Nancy turned her flashlight into old wardrobes and cupboards.

After an hour of strenuous work they had found nothing. Captain Easterly, weary and perspiring, called a halt.

As Bess dropped into a deck chair, her face streaked with dust, and her hair hanging in damp strings, she groaned, "I give up."

Even George looked discouraged, but Nancy was eager to continue the search.

"The crew's sleeping quarters are next," she said. "They must have had a lot of time on their hands in the forecastle," Nancy reflected. "Lying in their bunks thinking of nothing in particular, the men might have carved things on the timbers of the hull."

George, her interest rekindled, started for the companionway. "Let's have a look," she said.

Bess closed her eyes and leaned back. "You can tell me about it," she said.

They left her on deck and went below with the captain. The forecastle had a musty smell, but it was cool.

Nancy and George turned their flashlights on the seasoned old timbers. "Just look at the things cut into the wood!" George exclaimed.

There were initials and names, hearts and anchors, and the roughly carved outlines of a woman's face.

"Here it is!" Nancy cried out. *"Dream of Melissa*—all spelled out." She held her light on the spot and Captain Easterly stared.

"It's as plain as the nose on your face," he said eagerly. "So this old clipper really is the *Dream of Melissa!*"

Nancy smiled at the skipper. "Now it won't be hard to clear up the title."

Captain Easterly looked thoughtful. "I don't know. Maybe we'll find out somebody other than Mr. Farnsworth owns the clipper, and won't sell it to me." The man heaved a great sigh. "I'd sure hate to lose her at this point. I've grown mighty fond of the *Bonny Scot.*"

Nancy felt that she should get in touch with her father at once, and said she would go ashore to telephone him, as well as notify the police that Flip Fay had been aboard.

"Maybe Dad came across the name *Dream of Melissa* in his search," she added.

Bess and George went with her. Mr. Drew was just leaving his River Heights office to go to court, but he waited to hear his daughter's astounding report.

"Fine work, my dear," he said. "Yes, I came upon a record of the *Dream of Melissa* but not her captain's name. Hold on. I'll see if I have any notes on her." The lawyer left the telephone a few minutes. When he came back, he said, "The *Dream of Melissa* is listed as a lost clipper belonging to the Eastern Shore Shipping Company. I'll get in touch with them at once and wire you what they say."

When Nancy hung up, she repeated the conversation to Bess and George. After calling State Police headquarters to report on The Crow, the girls bought some fresh vegetables, fruit, and a steak. Returning to the clipper, they found Captain Easterly dozing in his chair on deck. He opened one eye.

"Anything new?" he asked. "Did you get your father, Nancy?"

Upon hearing that the ship originally had belonged to the Eastern Shore Shipping Company, the elderly man became glum. He was sure they soon would put him off the clipper.

"Dad will fix things up," Nancy told him encouragingly. "Don't worry."

She watched eagerly for someone to deliver a telegram. About two o'clock the captain pointed over the port rail. A rowboat was approaching the clipper. At the oars was a boy in faded blue overalls. The three girls leaned on the rail, and as he came close, Nancy called:

"Ahoy there!"

"Miss Nancy Drew here?" the boy asked.

"I'm Nancy Drew."

The youngster rested on the oars. "I've got a telegram and a package for you," he said.

Nancy dropped a line over the side, and the boy tied the box to it, with the telegram under the string, and watched her haul it up. Then he started to row away.

"Wait!" Nancy called, seeing no sender's name on the package. "Who sent the box?"

"I dunno," the boy answered with a shrug. He rowed quickly back toward shore.

The captain, who had now come to the rail, looked curiously at the parcel. "You must have an admirer, Nancy," he teased.

Nancy smiled. "Dad must have ordered a surprise," she said, turning the box over. "He's always— Oh, my goodness!"

On the bottom of the box, crudely drawn in

heavy black pencil, were a skull and crossbones!

"Be careful," Captain Easterly said quickly. "This doesn't look like a friendly gift."

Suddenly they heard a faint sound of movement inside the pasteboard.

Bess drew back. "Nancy," she whispered, "it's something alive. Look at the little air holes in the end."

Nancy borrowed the captain's knife and gingerly cut the string. As she opened the box, Bess screamed.

A green lizard lifted its head and flicked its tiny tongue.

"Don't touch that thing!" Captain Easterly shouted. "It means death!"

CHAPTER XV

Hidden Treasure

CAPTAIN Easterly seized the box, clapped the lid on, and threw it overboard. Breathing hard, he watched it toss about a few seconds, then start to sink. He turned to the astonished girls, a sheepish expression on his face.

"I suppose you'll think I'm a superstitious old man when you learn why I did that. We men of the sea pick up some strange stories. There's one in the Far East that if a certain kind of lizard crawls toward a man he's doomed to die."

"Oh, how dreadful!" Bess quavered. "Nancy, we'd better leave right away!"

"Don't be silly," George scolded her cousin. "Why, that poor little lizard was as harmless as a mouse. Anyway, this isn't the Far East."

"Maybe the telegram will explain who sent it," said Nancy, ripping open the envelope.

Nancy read aloud the message which proved to

be from her father and had no connection with the package. Mr. Drew had had a long telephone conversation with Mr. Ogden of the Eastern Shore Shipping Company. Mr. Ogden had been amazed to learn their long-lost clipper, the *Dream of Melissa,* had turned up. He was coming from Maryland in a few days to find out about it. He would be very appreciative if Captain Easterly remained in charge and Nancy and her friends stayed with him.

"That settles it, Bess," George spoke up when Nancy read the instructions. "We're staying. You know what I'm going to do? Hunt up that boy who brought the lizard and make him tell me who gave him the job of delivering it."

"I'll bet it was either Flip Fay or old Grizzle Face," Bess asserted.

Captain Easterly had walked off a distance. He stood looking southward. Nancy knew he felt sad about the turn of events. She guessed that he was afraid of legal difficulties in connection with buying the clipper, and that the company would put a price on it which he could not afford to pay.

"I'm sure Dad will come back on this case as soon as he can, and work things out," Nancy told him.

To get the captain's mind off his worry, George added, "Why don't we get to work on your cabin, Captain, and repair some of that damage?"

"You girls are a tonic for an old fellow," he

said, smiling. "I'll do the work myself, and you girls solve the mysteries."

Nancy's eyes danced with excitement. "I'm going to Provincetown. The *Dream of Melissa* sailed from there on her last known voyage, you recall."

The captain looked at her quizzically. "Think you can find somebody who's heard of her?"

"I'm going to try."

Bess remained aboard. As Nancy and George set off in the rowboat, Bess called, "Be careful, won't you?"

They promised. In town the girls separated. Nancy caught a bus for Provincetown.

As she rode along the beautiful coast in the bright summer afternoon, Nancy's brain was in a whirl of deductions about the *Dream of Melissa*. Someone in Provincetown must have been waiting for Captain Rogers to return. A sweetheart, a wife? Perhaps he had children. Would any of their descendants remember the story?

When she stepped from the bus, Nancy gasped in delight at the quaint old town. No wonder so many artists came here to paint the weathered houses, the flower gardens, the little shops, the old fishing boats tied up at the wharves.

Nancy did not know where to begin asking questions. Perhaps if she wandered along the water's edge she would meet someone who looked as though he might know a few answers.

The first person she came to was a white-haired man in a blue smock, seated on a canvas stool. He was sketching the outlines of a dilapidated shed. She watched him a moment.

"Do you paint, young lady?" he asked as he looked up, smiling.

"Not very well," Nancy confessed.

From that small beginning they entered into a conversation. The painter, John Singleton, told Nancy that he had been coming to Provincetown every summer for many, many years.

"Then you must know something of the town's history," Nancy said. "Did you ever hear of a clipper ship called the *Dream of Melissa?* Or of Captain Perry Rogers?"

The artist frowned, as if he were trying to remember something. "Seems to me old Mrs. Mathilda Smythe has a story about a Captain Rogers—or was it Roberts? Beats me. Why don't you go talk to Mrs. Smythe, anyway?"

"I will," Nancy said earnestly, and asked where she could find her.

The artist gave the address of the elderly widow and told Nancy to mention his name. Nancy found the gray-shingled cottage and knocked on the door. In a moment a fragile old lady of eighty opened it. Nancy introduced herself, and explained why she had come.

"Oh, yes," Mrs. Smythe said cordially. "Please come in."

Nancy followed her into the spotless parlor, and told her briefly about the *Dream of Melissa* and Captain Rogers.

"Captain Perry Rogers!" Mrs. Smythe exclaimed. "My mother nearly married him."

"Really?" Nancy was excited. "Please tell me the story, Mrs. Smythe."

The old woman sat forward in her rocking chair and cradled her hands in her lap.

"Captain Rogers fell in love with my mother, Mathilda Witherspoon," Mrs. Smythe said slowly. "She was only sixteen. Captain Rogers was a good bit older, and her family opposed the marriage. But Mother and the captain were very much in love. They planned to marry secretly as soon as he returned from the voyage to India."

"But he never came back?" Nancy asked.

Mrs. Smythe shook her head sadly. "My mother never heard from him again. She waited and waited, hoping some news would come. At last she married Father. And a fine man he was too, mind you."

"Did anyone ever learn anything about the ship?" Nancy asked. "Was the *Melissa* wrecked?"

"No one knows, Miss Drew. From that day to this, nobody has ever found a trace of the ship or her cargo."

The old lady rocked gently, looking into space. She pursed her lips and gave a little smile. Nancy felt she was about to be let in on a secret.

"Captain Rogers made Mother a promise."

"What sort of promise?" Nancy prompted.

"He said he would bring her back a priceless gift. She didn't know what it was. But Captain Rogers was a rich man. He made many profitable voyages to the Orient."

Nancy asked eagerly, "Didn't your mother ever guess what the gift might have been?"

"No, I'm afraid not. At any rate, in the stories I heard, the treasure was always something mysterious." She smiled wistfully. "Perhaps if the *Melissa* had returned, and Captain Rogers had married Mother, there would be money today to pay the taxes on this house. It's the old Witherspoon homestead, and I'm afraid I'm going to lose it."

Nancy longed to tell Mrs. Smythe of the *Bonny Scot*—that it was almost certainly the long-lost *Dream of Melissa*. But she did not want to raise the woman's hopes of finding Captain Rogers' fabulous gift.

She did tell her, however, about the snuffbox with the initials P. R., and how it had led her to the story of Captain Rogers and his ship.

"If I ever find that snuffbox again," Nancy promised Mrs. Smythe, "I'll bring it here to show you."

She said good-by and hurried to catch a bus back to meet George. She could scarcely wait to tell her and the others aboard the clipper that there really had been a treasure on the *Dream of Melissa.*

"And no doubt it's still there!" Nancy finished telling George as the two girls rowed back to the ship.

"And if we don't look out, the thieves will find it before we do," George said seriously. "Listen to this."

She said that through the owner of the grocery-hardware store, she had located the boy who had delivered the lizard. At first he had not been willing to answer George's questions. But after being told that Captain Easterly thought there was a poisonous lizard in the box, the boy had talked freely, assuring George he had not known what was in the box.

"Big, tall guy I'd seen in the drugstore when I was gettin' a soda, come up to me on the beach," the boy said. "Told me he wanted to play a joke on a girl on the *Bonny Scot*. Paid me well for taking the box."

George said he had not learned the name of the man who had been hanging around town, so she had accompanied the boy on a tour of the streets to find him. Having no luck, they went to the drugstore. George had learned from the description that the suspect had had a prescription filled under the name of Lane.

"Lane!" Nancy exclaimed. "The man who kidnapped Captain Easterly!"

"I'm afraid so," George said. "Our enemies are closing in!"

When Captain Easterly heard all the stories, he became very much excited. "Those pirates won't get the better of us!" the skipper shouted. "Nancy, that treasure is still on the clipper. Rogers hid it so well nobody could locate it. We're going to search her from stem to stern to find it!"

The skipper had no suggestions about where the treasure might be hidden. It would be an every-man-for-himself hunt.

"But first, I'm going ashore and hire a guard for the night, while you girls rustle up some supper," he told them.

He was not gone long, and when he returned, Captain Easterly said a detective would arrive about ten o'clock and cruise around in a boat during the night.

As soon as the supper dishes were washed, the girls were ready to start their search for Captain Rogers' treasure. The captain already was poking around in the hold.

"I was thinking," Bess said, "we haven't ever really taken the chart room apart."

"Now that's an idea I could work on!" George said. "Bess and I will take the chart room, Nancy, while you help the captain."

It seemed to Nancy that the likeliest spot for Captain Rogers to hide his treasure would be in his private quarters. When she reached the cabin, the door was ajar. She was tempted to hook it open, since it was a hot, still evening, but she had an uneasy feeling that someone might sneak up behind her while she was working. So Nancy closed the door behind her and snapped the catch.

With a sense of security, Nancy approached the built-in bookcase and began to remove the volumes from one section. Behind a South Sea Island manual she found a half-filled tobacco can. Not very exciting, she thought.

Next, Nancy removed the second section of books, and beamed her flashlight closely against the paneled wall. Something caught her eye; a small knot in the wood which stood out a quarter of an inch.

Quickly she removed it, inserted her forefinger in the knothole, and pulled gently on the panel. With a loud scraping sound it came loose. Behind the panel lay a carved box!

Nancy's heart was beating wildly. Was the treasure inside? She lifted the box. It was very heavy. Setting it on the bunk, Nancy lifted the lid and gasped.

Gold coins!

Excitedly she dumped the contents of the box

on the bunk. As she did so, she heard a click behind her, then a footstep.

Nancy wheeled—and stood speechless. Flip Fay was standing there!

He smirked, evidently pleased at the young detective's dilemma. The door was still closed and locked. It seemed as if The Crow had come through the wall!

"Let out one peep and it'll be your last!" Flip leered, shaking a fist.

With his eyes leveled upon Nancy, he quickly crossed the cabin and stood with his back against the door.

"Now before I take that treasure," he said, "I have a thing or two to say to you, Nancy Drew."

His impudent, drawling voice brought Nancy to her senses. She was more angry now than frightened. And she was determined to outwit him.

"I don't intend to let you take anything," she said coolly.

Nancy tossed her head in a gesture of defiance, but she was really looking desperately around the tiny cabin. If there were only a way of summoning help!

The man's lips curled in a crafty smile. "Don't act too smart, Nancy Drew. Because I got a little deal to make with you. If you and your friends don't squeal on me, I won't hurt you."

"And if we do?"

Flip Fay made an angry sound. "You'll regret it. Now move, so I can get that money."

In that moment Nancy had seen something which made her heart leap. Hanging inconspicuously against the wall, near the desk, was what looked like a bell cord!

As if obeying Flip Fay's command, Nancy moved away from the bunk. She leaned against the desk and pulled the cord. Was it in working order? Would it summon the captain—somebody —to her aid?

Flip Fay pawed through the coins as if he were looking for something else. He eyed Nancy once more.

"Open your hands!" he commanded. Seeing they were empty, he cried out, "You must have dropped it! You've tried to get the best of me for the last time!"

"What do you mean?" Nancy asked, sparring for time.

Fay glared at the girl, hate in his eyes. "Maybe you think I don't know who told the police about me in River Heights, and again in Boston. You found my ring."

"You stole Mrs. Marvin's jewelry," Nancy retorted.

"What if I did? That's peanuts compared to the prize on this old tub."

Fay hurriedly put the coins into the box. He seemed to be thinking, trying to decide on something. How Nancy wished she could read his thoughts! Once more she pulled the old bell cord.

"No," Flip Fay said aloud, as if answering a question in his mind. "You're smart, Nancy Drew, but not smart enough for me. You'll never find out how I come and go on this ship."

"Why not?"

Nancy wished she could trick him into telling.

"You and your blundering old captain are going to be left with your mouths hanging open," Fay bragged.

Nancy answered quietly, "Even if you don't tell me, it won't do you a bit of good. You think you'll escape, but that's where you're wrong. The police are after you, Flip Fay—in River Heights, in Boston, and here on Cape Cod too."

She saw his fists tighten. He made an ugly sound.

"The police know you're wanted for West Coast robberies," she continued. "You're The Crow, and they're combing this state for you. Maybe they won't get you today. But they'll get you tomorrow or the next day."

Nancy would have kept on talking—anything to gain time. But there were quick footsteps in the passageway outside. Fay clamped a heavy hand on Nancy's shoulder. The other hand closed against her throat.

"Not a word—d'you hear?" he whispered hoarsely.

Someone tried the locked door, then knocked. "Nancy, are you all right? Nancy—?"

It was George. She had come in answer to her friend's summons! If only Nancy could speak to her! But Fay's hand tightened threateningly.

George tried the door again, hesitated, then hurried away.

Flip Fay stepped back. "See what I mean?" He gave Nancy a leering smile. "You girls are no match for Flip Fay. So you'd better think over what I told you. Call off the police. Tell 'em you made a mistake—or take the consequences!"

"I'll—I'll do as I please," Nancy gasped. "This ship is being guarded. If you try to escape—"

"You'll do as I tell you, Nancy Drew, and give me the ruby!"

Desperate, the young detective had been edging toward the door. She must distract his attention and get out.

"The treasure!" she cried suddenly, pointing toward the gold coins.

Fay whirled around. In that split second Nancy turned the key in the lock.

CHAPTER XVI

A Trap Door

THE next moment Nancy turned the door handle and darted into the passageway.

"Captain Easterly!" she yelled at the top of her voice.

George came running. "What's the matter? I heard a bell before, but I—"

"Get the captain—quick!"

But the skipper had heard Nancy's frantic cry, and now appeared, panting for breath. Suspecting trouble, he had picked up a belaying pin.

"Flip Fay's in your cabin!" Nancy exclaimed.

"In my cabin, eh? We'll soon fix him!"

The captain flung open the door and poised the belaying pin.

"All right, Fay!" he growled. "Come out peaceably."

There was no answer.

"Stay here," the skipper ordered the girls. He strode in. "Empty!" he exclaimed.

Nancy and George hurried inside the cabin. Nancy opened the wardrobe. No one was hiding there. The captain opened his locker. That, too, was empty. The portholes were fastened shut on the inside.

The old mariner stood in the middle of the cabin, rubbing the side of his face. Nancy looked about the room with growing excitement. There must be some secret means of escape from the cabin. Flip knew about it.

Nancy's sharp eyes traveled over the paneled walls, along the floor. She could see no sign of a trap door. Her glance fell on the mahogany wardrobe with renewed interest.

"Captain," she said, "have you ever moved this wardrobe?"

"No. It was built in that position, nailed down. Why do you ask?"

"I wonder what's under it."

Nancy poked her head inside, examining the sturdy floor.

"Look!" she exulted, putting her finger through a small metal ring and raising the entire wardrobe floor, which was hinged from underneath.

"Well, I'll be hornswoggled!" Captain Easterly cried, reaching for his flashlight. The glow revealed a ladder leading down into complete darkness. "This must go to the hold," he said, "but I don't understand how we missed it."

"Maybe Fay's hiding down there," Nancy suggested. She listened and thought she heard a creaking noise. "I'm going after him!"

"Not so fast," Captain Easterly said. "Remember, Fay is a criminal, and if he's at the foot of this ladder he has the advantage of anyone coming down."

At that moment Bess came running along the passageway. "Captain Easterly," she cried, "my ruby's gone!"

"Ruby?" the captain repeated. "What ruby?"

"She means that pendant with the imitation ruby," Nancy explained. "Are you sure it's not in the cabin, Bess?"

"Of course I'm sure. I took it off a little while ago and laid it on the chest. I just went back there, and it's gone."

"Well, what of it?" George scoffed. "We have something more important to think about."

"It might all tie in," Nancy said excitedly. "Tell you my idea later."

As Bess stared openmouthed, Nancy followed Captain Easterly down the ladder. It was short, and at the foot was a narrow passageway. Ten feet ahead was a sliding panel, cleverly concealed in a thin wall. It opened into the forecastle.

"Watch yourself," the captain said as he slid the panel back. "That rat may be waitin' for us."

But Fay was not in sight, and an open porthole ahead gave mute evidence he had made his escape from the ship. Nancy ran to the front of the crew's quarters to look out the opening. In the dusk she could see no one.

"If he's swimming, we ought to be able to catch him in the dinghy," Nancy said excitedly. "Come on, Captain Easterly!"

The two rowed to shore, but Flip Fay had outwitted them. Furthermore, he had taken the box of coins with him. Angrily the captain reported the incident to the State Police, then he and Nancy started back to the *Bonny Scot*. On the way, Nancy said to him:

"That box of coins was very heavy. How could Fay dive overboard with it?"

"I noticed a life preserver missing from my cabin," the captain replied. "Guess he tied the box to it and threw it overboard, then dragged it along as he swam."

Nancy was discouraged. The treasure was gone and the thief had escaped.

But there was one gleam of hope. Surely Captain Perry Rogers had not been bringing his sweetheart a box of gold coins. Mrs. Smythe had said the gift was fabulous. Flip Fay had acted as if he thought Nancy were holding a ruby in her hand. The fabulous gift, no doubt! He certainly had not had time to search for it before leaving the ship!

"Pretty clever, whoever designed the *Bonny Scot*," Captain Easterly observed. "I mean, that secret ladder and passageway leading down from my quarters to the fo'c'sle. The floor of the passageway was a false ceiling in the hold and was never discovered."

When Bess and George heard the captain repeat his remark a few minutes later, as they all seated themselves in comfortable chairs on deck, Bess asked why the secret compartment had been put there in the first place.

Captain Easterly thought perhaps the early captains of the clipper liked to spy on their crews. A captain could leave his cabin by this ladder when the crew thought he was sound asleep, and see what they were up to.

"I'll bet he was surprised at some of the things he heard about himself." George laughed.

"The captain could get wind of a mutiny in time to stop it," Easterly went on.

"Oh, Bess," said Nancy as he fell silent, "did you find your pendant with the ruby?"

"No. I'm sure that awful Fay took it." Nancy said she thought Fay had been watching his chance, and when Bess laid the pendant down, he had taken it.

"He must be pretty silly," George remarked. "Surely he must know it's not a real ruby."

Nancy wondered if Flip had not had some other reason for taking the synthetic gem. While she was trying to figure it out, a voice from the water called, "Ahoy up there!" For a moment the group was startled, but the newcomer proved to be the detective reporting for guard duty.

"Fine, fine!" Captain Easterly boomed over the rail. "Now we can have a good night's rest. But blow that whistle of yours if you need any help."

The night proved to be peaceful, however. Refreshed and eager to start work, Nancy announced at breakfast that she had a hunch Captain Perry Rogers' fabulous gift was still hidden aboard ship. She was sure if there had been anything else in the box of coins, except money, she would have seen it.

"If you don't mind, Captain Easterly, I want to search your cabin further," Nancy said.

"Go right ahead. It wouldn't surprise me if the place is full of treasures. I'll keep guard on deck so none of those scoundrels can climb aboard again."

Bess and George wanted to continue their search of the chart room. Nancy went off to the captain's quarters and set about making a thorough investigation of the old, built-in desk.

The mellowed wood, the type of hardware, the many old marks and scratches, and the well-worn edges made Nancy feel sure that this was the original desk. Perry Rogers, captain of the *Dream of Melissa,* must have used it.

The desk was built with shelves at the top on which Captain Easterly kept a few books. Beneath them was a broad cover which could be lowered for a writing surface. When this was closed, it concealed many small compartments. The lower part of the desk had three large drawers.

Nancy's attention was attracted to these drawers, which she pulled out and measured along the side of the desk.

The desk, she found, was several inches deeper than the drawers. Excited, Nancy reached to the back of the dusty openings. She felt the wood here and there.

In the back of the center drawer space, her fingers located a tiny panel. It moved!

CHAPTER XVII

The Long-Lost Clue

PUSHING the chair back from the desk, Nancy dropped to her knees and looked into the opening.

She could move the little panel back and forth, but behind it was a solid piece of wood. No secret compartment? This was disappointing. She had been almost certain she had uncovered the hiding place of Captain Rogers' fabulous gift.

As she slid the panel again, feeling carefully for a hidden spring, Bess and George burst into the room. Their faces were smudged. Bess sneezed.

"Oh, that terrible dusty chart room!"

"Never mind the dust," George said, brushing a stray wisp of hair from her forehead with the back of her hand. "See what we found jammed behind a drawer, Nancy!" George offered her a small chart, tightly rolled.

Nancy unrolled it gingerly. It was very brittle.

"Here, put it on the floor," George suggested.

Nancy did so. Then, with three pairs of hands holding the edges of the chart, Nancy gazed at a strange map showing the islands of the East Indies. A penciled line meandered from Calcutta through the waters of the Orient, ending abruptly near Java.

Another part of the puzzle of the clipper jogged into place in Nancy's mind. "The return trip of the *Dream of Melissa!*" she exclaimed. "Captain Rogers charted his ship's course until something happened to stop him. Bess, find Captain Easterly. We must show him this."

When Bess left, Nancy told George of the secret compartment in the desk.

"Let me try," George suggested. "Perhaps I can open it."

She was working at it when Bess returned with the skipper.

"What's this I hear about a chart, Nancy?" Captain Easterly demanded.

Nancy showed it to him. The captain had never seen it before, but he agreed with Nancy that it was probably part of the log of the *Melissa*'s fateful journey. Then Nancy showed him the drawer in the desk.

"I know that desk better than I know my own mind," he said. "You won't find anything hidden in there."

"But look, Captain," Nancy pleaded, picking

up the drawer. "See how much deeper the desk is than this drawer. There must be something back of it."

His eyebrows went up. "Well," he said, "I never knew that." He put an arm into the opening and found the little movable panel. "Hah! Oriental contraption. Take you a week of Sundays to figure it out."

"Let's use a hammer and chisel instead," George put in. "Why bat our brains out over this thing when we could just chop into it?"

Nancy objected. "The ship belongs to the Eastern Shore Shipping Company," she reminded them. "We have no right to destroy the desk. Let's work on the movable panel a little longer."

The captain smiled. "You just want to see if you can outwit the man who made the compartment, Nancy."

He and Bess each took a turn, but with no better luck than George had had.

"It'll take you all day," Bess told Nancy. "Meanwhile, George, we'd better pick up the wreckage we left in the chart room, before the ship's master sees it."

The two girls left. Captain Easterly dropped into his armchair, and Nancy continued to experiment with the puzzle behind the desk drawer. The moving panel, she thought, must be a key to the next panel. If one got it in exactly the right position, something else would move.

Patiently she tried. Her knees ached, and her neck was stiff, but she kept wiggling the little piece of wood back and forth.

Then suddenly she felt something give! Another panel had slid open. Captain Easterly watched with excitement.

Eagerly Nancy worked with this second key to the mysterious compartment. The skipper hung over her, urging her on. It took some time, but eventually a third panel moved, and Nancy was electrified to find her fingers slipping into an opening.

"I've got it!" she cried out.

Captain Easterly went into the passageway and bellowed for the other girls. By the time they came running in, Nancy had put her hand on something that felt like paper.

Gingerly she drew it out, yellow and crumbling. They all crowded around her.

"There's writing on it," Bess whispered, her eyes popping.

The faded ink showed a hasty but elegant hand, with long curlicues.

"It's signed by Captain Perry Rogers!" Nancy said in awe.

"What does it say?" Captain Easterly fumbled for the glasses in his shirt pocket.

Nancy read slowly. "It's addressed to Josiah Ogden, and it says:

" 'Honorable Sir: I have the misfortune to inform you we are beset by pirates. Their names are unknown to me. Should God will my decease, I pray thee, search my beloved lady of wood and therein find a precious ruby to be presented in person to her whom I hoped to make my wife, Mathilda Witherspoon, as a lasting protestation of my devotion. Your humble servant, Perry Rogers.' "

Bess gasped. "A letter from Captain Perry Rogers himself—after all these years!" She felt the paper as if she could not believe it was real. "A ruby for his sweetheart!"

"What did he mean by 'my beloved lady of wood'?" George wondered. She looked quickly around the cabin walls at the figurines. "These?"

The captain followed her glance. "Those little carved figures came with the ship," he said. "I believe Rogers had them here in his day."

"What are we waiting for?" George demanded.

They were such lovely little figures that no one wanted to break them apart, and yet if they hoped to find the "precious ruby" Captain Rogers had referred to, it seemed they would have to.

Bess was carefully tapping Venus to see if she sounded hollow, when she stopped abruptly. "Nancy," she complained, "you haven't said a word. And you aren't searching. Say, do you suppose Flip Fay thought my ruby pendant was the famous treasure?"

"No, I don't," Nancy answered. "He's a jewel thief. He'd know a fake ruby in a moment. I have a hunch Flip thought he could fool old Grizzle Face with it, though."

"Why?" George wanted to know.

"To keep him off the ship—so he couldn't find the real treasure."

Further conversation was halted by the far-away shout of "Ship ahoy!"

"Who's that?" Bess asked uneasily.

"Not one of Flip's friends," George decided. "They never announce their arrival."

Nancy was in the lead as they made their way to the deck. A tall, middle-aged man was rowing to the side of the *Bonny Scot*. They tossed him a rope ladder and he pulled himself over the deck rail with much effort.

"I'm Josiah Ogden," he said after he ceased puffing. "And I suppose you're Easterly."

Josiah Ogden! The name of the man to whom Perry Rogers had addressed his note!

Recovering from her surprise, Nancy recalled that her father had said a Mr. Ogden would come from Maryland in a few days. He must be a direct descendant of the other Josiah Ogden.

"Which one of you girls is Nancy Drew?" the man asked.

"I am."

"Glad to know you," Ogden said, putting out his hand. "Smart father you've got. And"—he grinned—"I understand that you're pretty smart yourself!"

Nancy flushed and did not answer. She did not like his breezy manner.

Captain Easterly seemed too dumfounded to speak. He had not expected Mr. Ogden so soon. Too many things had happened too fast!

"Will you sit down?" the captain finally found words. "Well, Mr. Ogden, what's the company going to do? I hope they'll let me buy the *Bonny Scot*."

"*Dream of Melissa*," the man corrected him. "I'm afraid not, Captain Easterly. My instructions are to take charge here at once."

"You mean—" Nancy gasped.

"That the four of you are to leave this morning."

"But, Mr. Ogden, this is the captain's home! He's lived on this ship for two years! You just can't put Captain Easterly off like—like—"

"You're trespassing on private property," Ogden said firmly. "I'm taking charge of the ship, and I'm asking all of you to leave—as soon as possible!"

CHAPTER XVIII

The Sailor's Tale

THE ruddy, weather-beaten face of Captain Easterly grew pale. His usually bombastic mood was
completely gone.

"All right, Mr. Ogden," he said. "We'll leave
the ship. Come on, girls. Let's pack up."

"I'm sure Dad will work things out, Captain,"
Nancy whispered as they started down the companionway.

"I just hate to leave," George mourned.

Bess did not share George's gloom. "We'll be
a lot safer on land." She sighed, then put a con-
soling hand on Nancy's arm. "Don't feel bad
that you can't solve the mystery. You made a fine
try."

Nancy smiled. She was sure the case was not
over and had not given up. The girls packed their
suitcases. Finally Nancy clicked hers shut and sat
down.

" 'Search my beloved lady of wood!' " she said quietly, repeating the message Captain Rogers had written. "Doesn't that ring a bell, girls?"

The cousins exchanged glances and shook their heads.

"The wooden lady," Nancy went on, "probably was the figurehead of the *Dream of Melissa,* and the ruby's in it!"

"Hypers!" George shouted. "You've got it!"

"Oh, Nancy, you're wonderful!" Bess exclaimed. "But—but where *is* the wooden lady? I hope for your sake it's still in existence."

"Even if the ship belongs to the Eastern Shore Shipping Company, the ruby doesn't," George declared.

"It isn't ours either—it's Mrs. Smythe's," Nancy reminded her friends. "Oh, it would be so nice if we could find it for her! She needs the money. Anyway, it's clear what we must do."

"You mean look for that figurehead?" asked George.

Nancy nodded.

"But that will be like looking for a needle in a haystack," objected Bess.

"Maybe not," said Nancy. "If the company doesn't know where it is, old Grizzle Face may. He evidently knows a lot about this ship."

"Are you going to tell Captain Easterly?" asked George.

"I'd rather do some looking first. I don't want

to disappoint him—he has enough troubles. And now, let's hurry!"

Before leaving the clipper, Nancy spoke to Mr. Ogden. "When you restore the ship, are you going to put the figurehead back on?"

"The what?" he asked blankly. "Oh, yes. I suppose we'll put on something."

"Not the original?"

Mr. Ogden looked at Nancy searchingly. "It's gone, unless maybe you know something about it."

"No, I don't. I was just wondering if *you* did."

Two small boats went ashore. One carried the girls and their baggage. The other was loaded with Captain Easterly and his personal belongings. At the beach Mr. Ogden tied one boat to the other, then rowed back to the *Bonny Scot.*

"Pretty note this is!" Captain Easterly stormed. "As soon as I get located, I'm going to tell that Eastern Shore Shipping Company a thing or two!" Then suddenly his mood changed and he chuckled. He tapped his pocket. "I've got Captain Perry Rogers' note in here. Maybe that'll make 'em come to terms."

"Let us know what you find out," Nancy said.

She gave him the address of a guesthouse in town where she and the girls planned to stay. The captain went storming off to find someone to transport his belongings.

Nancy and her friends unpacked in a sunny

bedroom of the guesthouse, and discussed the problem of finding the figurehead.

"First, we must locate old Grizzle Face," Nancy decided. "And I've just one clue to where he might be."

"What's that?" Bess asked.

"Remember when he took that snuffbox away from me, down on the beach? I noticed something on the lapel of his coat. It looked like an art exhibit button."

George hooted. "Hypers!" He's no artist, Nancy."

"I don't mean he's an artist," explained Nancy. "But he could be an artist's model."

"With that beard he'd make a wonderful model," Bess admitted. "I'd like to paint him myself."

"And if he models," concluded Nancy, "I know where we're likely to find him. In Provincetown."

Nancy and her friends decided to hire a car and go to Provincetown immediately. They left a note at the guesthouse for Captain Easterly, telling him where they were going.

"It feels good to be driving," said Nancy as they sped along the sandy coast. "I've missed it."

When they reached Provincetown, they had a hasty lunch. Then Nancy telephoned John Singleton, the artist who had directed her to Mathilda Smythe. She described the grizzle-bearded sailor and asked if he ever posed for local artists.

"Indeed he does. I've painted him myself," said Mr. Singleton. "One of my portraits—'Old Man of the Sea'—won a prize. Want to locate him?"

Nancy said she did, and Mr. Singleton named a studio fronting the harbor. It proved to be an old fishing shack converted into a classroom by a group of young art students. On a raised platform at the back of the room sat the grizzle-bearded Red Quint, his right hand shielding his eyes as if he were looking out over the sea. Nancy walked over to the instructor.

"I'm sorry to interrupt, but I want to speak to your model. When will the class be over?"

The art teacher glanced at his watch. "It's over now."

He called to Red Quint, and the bearded sailor came shambling over. He stopped short upon seeing the girls.

"How'd you know I was here?" he asked.

Nancy did not answer the question. "Come outside to our car," she said. "We want to talk to you."

The three girls led him to the car, which Nancy had parked in front of the studio. Quint twisted his hands nervously.

"I haven't done nuthin' wrong."

"Oh, no," said George sarcastically. "You only kidnapped Captain Easterly, and . . ."

Quint's utter astonishment seemed to prove his innocence.

"But you knew about it?" Nancy asked.

"Not a thing."

"But you were a stowaway."

"When I knew you was goin' to leave Boston, I had to stay aboard," the sailor said doggedly, "so's I could keep my eye on the ship."

He also admitted he had shut Nancy in the wardrobe, and taken some food, and locked Bess in the galley closet, and hacked at the captain's quarters and the hold. But he had not been responsible for the fire nor the severe damage to Easterly's cabin.

"Then the other stowaway was," Nancy said. "Who was he?"

Quint hung his head and did not answer.

Nancy prodded him. "It was Fay or Lane."

Grizzle Face winced. "It was Fay. Never heard of Lane."

"You telephoned Fay in Boston," Nancy said, "and told him where the *Bonny Scot* was."

The sailor admitted it. He leaned against the car door. The man seemed suddenly old, tired, and beaten.

"What were you looking for on the *Bonny Scot?*" Nancy asked him.

"A ruby. There was supposed to be a priceless ruby hidden on board."

The girls pretended to show surprise. "Did

your friend Flip Fay know about the ruby?"
Nancy asked.

Red Quint growled, "That double-crosser!
Came snoopin' around, tryin' to buy me off. A
fine friend he turned out to be, after I told him
the secret of the old ship!"

"What did he do?" Nancy asked.

"Cheated me—that's what," the old man cried
out. "I heard the *Bonny Scot* was tied up in Boston, so I went there to see if she was the ship I
knew about. I used to sneak aboard to search for
the ruby. About ten days ago Fay started hangin'
around the waterfront, and he got me talkin'."

Quint went on to say that he had foolishly told
Fay about the secret ladder on the old clipper and
the hidden ruby. "That double-crosser tried to
palm off a red stone on me last night. Told me it
was the real ruby, and he'd found it. But when
I got it in a good light, I knew it was a fake."

"That's why Flip Fay took my pendant!" Bess
spoke up. "Just like you said, Nancy! Do you still
have it?" she asked Red Quint.

As the man searched his pockets and handed
over the stone from Bess's pendant, Nancy asked
him, "How did you find out about the ruby and
the hidden ladder?"

"Somebody told me—somebody who knew.
Years ago, I signed up on a freighter in the South
Pacific. We laid up for repairs, one time, at some
island. Near Java, 'twas. There was an old man I

met there. He'd served on a pirate ship as a young fellow. He told me quite a story."

"What?" Nancy asked.

"In Bombay one of the pirate crew found out a precious ruby had been bought and taken on board a clipper called the *Dream of Melissa.*

"The pirates followed the ship, boarded her, and killed the captain and crew. Then they changed the clipper's name to *Bonny Scot.* The pirates combed every inch of her, lookin' for that ruby. But they never found it."

"What happened to the old *Melissa?*" asked George.

Red Quint shrugged. "The pirate crew mutinied. Some was killed, and the fellow I met was badly cut up. He holed in at that island for the rest of his life."

"It didn't pay him to be a pirate," Bess remarked.

Red Quint shook his head. "He was poor as a sand crab when I knew him. He said he never did get any of that pirate loot they talked about. All he found was a snuffbox. Before I left, he sold it to me."

Nancy asked thoughtfully, "Have you ever heard of a figurehead like the lady carved on that snuffbox?"

"Sure have," answered Red Quint. "Friend o' mine told me."

Quint's remark made Nancy's pulse pound.

Her hunch had been right! Quint did know something about the figurehead.

"Where is the figurehead, Mr. Quint?"

"I'm not telling!"

"I had hoped you'd cooperate with us," Nancy said kindly. "You'll need friends. Captain Easterly is going to press a charge of kidnapping. You'll have a hard time explaining how he happened to be at your boardinghouse."

Quint gulped. He scratched his head as he thought this over. Deciding he would like to have Nancy on his side in the event of an FBI investigation, he said, "All right, Miss Drew. I can't give you very good directions about where the figurehead is. I'll have to show you."

Nancy felt that he wanted to go along to find out why they were so eager to locate Melissa. There was nothing to do but take him. They all got into the car, and the sailor directed Nancy.

On the way, she asked him if he knew where Flip Fay was and if he had heard Fay was a wanted criminal known as The Crow. Quint did not know this. He thought Fay had skipped out.

They had left Provincetown when the girls noticed a car following them.

George peered out the back window. "It's a State Police car. The trooper's signaling for us to stop."

Nancy pulled over to the side of the road. The

other car stopped. A uniformed officer got out and put his head into the window of Nancy's automobile. He looked Red Quint over, then he said:

"You're under arrest. Come along with me!"

CHAPTER XIX

A Fiendish Plot

NANCY felt sheepish. She suddenly remembered having told the police to arrest Red Quint!

"A man answering this one's description is wanted on a disorderly conduct complaint," the trooper said. "The complaint was lodged by somebody named Nancy Drew."

"I'm Nancy Drew," the young detective said.

"You! Then what are you—? Say! All of you come along with me!"

The officer got into his car, taking Quint with him, and told Nancy to follow in her car. But as she trailed the trooper toward State Police headquarters, Nancy's brain was in a whirl. She had wanted Quint arrested. Perhaps now, out of spite, he would never reveal the whereabouts of the wooden lady!

When they arrived at headquarters, Nancy told the officers about Fay, Lane, and the abduction of Captain Easterly.

"I don't want to press my charge against Red Quint," she concluded. "I'm sure he's not a thief like the other two. But maybe he'd be better off in jail for his own protection. I don't know what Flip Fay might do to him if he found out how much Quint has told us."

The police captain seemed to think this was a fair proposition. Meanwhile, he said, they would check the sailor's story and speed up the search for Flip "The Crow" Fay.

Suddenly Quint, who had been listening quietly, said, "Could I speak to Miss Drew in private?"

The officer agreed. Nancy and Quint went off to a corner.

"Miss Drew," Grizzle Face whispered, "you've been square with me. I want to be square with you, so I'll tell you where the figurehead is. You take the road to Truro, but turn off just before at the sign that says Wright's Cove. About a mile the other side of a settlement, you'll find a little white house with an old sea trawler rotting away in the front yard. That's Mrs. Parker's house. That's the place."

Nancy thanked him, and the three girls hurried out to their car.

"Do you think Quint told you the truth?" Bess asked, worried. "Maybe he's just putting us off the scent so he can find the treasure himself when he gets out of jail."

"I think he's telling the truth," Nancy said.

It was a beautiful drive, but the girls scarcely noticed the trim cottages, the gardens, the blue sea and sky, as they sped on their way to the hiding place of the figurehead. Nancy finally turned down a sandy lane.

"There it is!" George cried. "White house, old fishing boat. There's a sign—Mrs. Parker's Guesthouse."

The girls jumped out of the car and ran up the brick walk. At that moment a woman came around from the back yard, carrying a hoe.

Nancy told her what they were looking for. "Is the figurehead here?" she asked.

"Oh, that old thing." Mrs. Parker smiled. "It's out in the woodshed. A man named Burns brought it here with him. . . . No, it was Mr. Bleeker, I guess. He owed me twelve weeks' board, and the poor man didn't have a cent. He offered me the figurehead in place of the money. Said I could sell it, but I never bothered."

How glad Nancy was that Mrs. Parker had not sold Melissa!

"Are you girls collecting antiques?" Mrs. Parker went on. "I have some Sandwich glass, if you'd like to look at that."

"No, we're just interested in the figurehead," Nancy told her, smiling. "May we see it, please?"

"Certainly." Mrs. Parker, still carrying the hoe, and quite unaware of her visitors' excitement and impatience, led the girls through the garden to the woodshed.

She unhooked the door, and they stepped over the sill into semidarkness. "It's behind these boxes," the woman said, pushing them aside.

Nancy helped her, and presently in the dim light she saw the long-lost figure of Melissa. The wooden lady was indeed like the carved lady on the snuffbox. The three girls picked up Melissa and carried her into the yard.

"She's beautiful," Bess said. "She must have looked lovely on the ship."

"Mr. Burns—or was it Bleeker?" Mrs. Parker explained, "told me the thing came off a pirate ship, but I don't believe those old yarns. I've heard too many of 'em."

The girls exchanged glances. Was her former boarder a descendant of a pirate? Had he removed the ruby from it? Hardly likely, or he would have been able to pay his rent.

"Would you sell the figurehead?" Nancy asked.

"Of course I'll sell it. What would you give for it?"

A bargain was quickly made, since Mrs. Parker was glad to get rid of Melissa. The girls carried the wooden lady to the car, and with some manipulating managed to get it inside. Then Nancy drove back quickly to the guesthouse where the girls were staying.

Their hostess was amused to see that they had

found an old figurehead. She had no objection to their taking Melissa upstairs.

"I can't wait," George kept saying. "Let's cut her right open and look for the ruby!"

They had just closed their door when the telephone in the lower hall rang. A moment later the owner of the house knocked on the girls' door.

"A message for you from Captain Easterly, Miss Drew," she said, coming in. "You're to follow him to the *Bonny Scot* at once. He'll leave a rented rowboat on shore for you."

Nancy was amazed. "Was that all?" she asked.

"He said he was moving back." The woman hesitated as though she did not want to reveal the rest of the message. In a moment the reason was clear. She was about to lose three boarders! "The captain said you were to move back, too."

"Then we'll have to go," Nancy said. "I'm sorry. We'll pay the full day's rent."

Once more the girls packed, then drove to the beach with Melissa. The promised rowboat was there. A slip of paper with Nancy's name printed on it lay on the floor. George offered to return the rented car. While she was gone, Nancy and Bess put Melissa and the luggage in the rowboat.

George soon returned, and they set out. Reaching the clipper, Nancy called to Captain Easterly. A moment later Mr. Ogden appeared.

"Hello, girls!" he said, smiling. "You got here ahead of the captain."

In the dim light Nancy saw the long-lost figurehead

"What made you change your mind?" Nancy asked.

Mr. Ogden said he had decided after they left that his company had been unduly hasty. He had telephoned his office and convinced his superiors to let Easterly buy the clipper.

"I had quite a time locating the captain," Mr. Ogden concluded, "but I did finally. Well, come aboard, girls. I see you picked up a figurehead."

He let down the rope ladder. George and Bess climbed up the side, then tossed down a rope which Nancy tied around the figurehead. They hauled Melissa aboard, while Nancy went up the ladder.

Mr. Ogden helped George and Bess carry the luggage to their former cabin. Nancy remained on deck to wait for Captain Easterly. She did not want to leave the figurehead for one minute!

In a few moments Bess returned. Excitedly she whispered that George hoped Nancy would begin hunting for the ruby at once. Mr. Ogden was in the captain's quarters, writing. George would keep track of him and warn the others if he came on deck.

"I think this is the place to start," said Nancy, eager to see if the ruby were still there. She pointed to a small block of wood forming a part of one shoulder. "This doesn't match the other shoulder," she pointed out.

Nancy ran to the stern of the ship where she

had seen a locker with tools. In a moment she came back with a chisel. With it, the girls quickly removed the odd block of wood.

"Goodness!" Bess cried, gaping at the hole below it.

In the hole lay a tiny metal box, rusted almost to paper thinness. Inside on a velvet lining was the precious ruby! The fabulous gem of the Orient glinted in the sunlight.

The girls were so excited that they did not hear stealthy footsteps behind them. Suddenly they were startled by a harsh, masculine voice.

"Thanks for all your footwork!"

Nancy and Bess whirled around to see Flip Fay smiling triumphantly!

"I'll take the ruby," he said, reaching for it.

Nancy held on tightly to the ruby, and ran for the rail, while Bess screamed and clutched at the thief.

Simultaneously Mr. Ogden appeared. Instead of assisting the girls, he suddenly laughed raucously. Pushing Bess to the deck, he helped The Crow overpower Nancy and took the ruby from her. "Fell right into our trap, didn't you?" Ogden gloated. "The smart Nancy Drew!"

"Stop the gab and get to work!" Fay ordered.

Nancy glared at Fay's companion. "I see now. You're not Josiah Ogden at all. You're Lane, the man who kidnapped Captain Easterly!"

The man smirked. "Anything else you want

to know?" he asked impudently as Fay produced some heavy rope.

In spite of the struggle they put up, the two girls were tied securely to the foremast. Then George, who had been locked in a closet, was brought up and bound also.

"You should have paid attention when you got my warning," Flip sneered, tying a final knot. "Easterly must have known what the lizard meant."

Lane spoke up. "If Farnsworth had let me buy the ship, you wouldn't be seein' land for the last time."

"What have you done with Captain Easterly?" Nancy asked her captors. She was sure now he, too, had been tricked.

The men looked at each other. Then Fay said enigmatically, "You might have a chance to say good-by to him yet."

With that, he and Lane walked quickly to the anchor windlass. With a sinking heart Nancy watched them haul up the anchor. Then they climbed over the rail.

"Have a nice trip," Flip Fay called as he disappeared from view. "The tide's going out, and there's a stiff breeze to take you to sea tonight."

"They've set us adrift!" Bess wailed as the girls struggled desperately to free themselves.

CHAPTER XX

Dreams Come True

NANCY wriggled and twisted to loosen the tight ropes which held her to the mast.

"Can you move your left hand, George?" Nancy asked.

"I can't move anything," George answered.

"We're drifting out of the cove!" Bess cried frantically. "We'll be lost at sea!"

They were indeed passing through the inlet, and the ship began to pitch and toss in the cross-currents. There was not another craft in sight to rescue the girls and darkness was fast closing in.

Something on the deck suddenly rolled toward them. Nancy saw that it was the chisel with which they had been working on the figurehead. If only she could reach it!

She yanked against the chafing ropes and worked her right foot loose. She had to wait for another roll of the ship to bring the chisel nearer. Finally she reached out, dragged the tool toward her, and held it with the toe of her shoe.

"How can you get it into your hand?" Bess asked, watching anxiously.

By this time Nancy had managed to free the lower part of her right arm. She wriggled and pulled, but she could not get close enough to the deck to pick up the chisel.

"If we could only manage to slide our ropes down on the mast," Nancy said.

"Let's all try," George urged. "We're tied together, so if one slides down, we've all got to."

Inch by inch the girls worked themselves down toward the deck, until at last Nancy grasped the chisel with her fingers. She began feverishly to work on the rope holding George's left arm, grinding the hemp against the mast with the cutting edge of the chisel.

"Hurry, Nancy!" Bess pleaded. "We're getting farther from shore every minute and soon it will be pitch black!"

George said encouragingly, "When we get loose, Nancy, do you suppose the three of us could hoist the foresail?"

Bess and Nancy looked at the great heavy loops of canvas. "It's our only chance to save ourselves," Nancy said. "And the wind's shifted, thank goodness."

Free at last, the three girls turned to the problem of raising the great sail to catch the night wind. With their combined strength they finally hoisted it, made the halyard fast, and rushed to the wheel. The canvas flapped furiously, the ship careened; and then, to their great relief, righted itself as the wind filled the great white sheet.

"We've done it!" Bess cried excitedly. "We're heading back toward the cove!"

"Can you girls manage without me?" Nancy asked.

"You aren't going to leave us?" Bess quavered.

Nancy said she had been mulling over Fay's remark about Captain Easterly. She was afraid it meant he was a prisoner on board.

"I want to look for him," she said.

"Go ahead," George told her. "We'll manage. Besides, there's a bit of a moon coming out, so at least we can see where we're going."

Nancy hurried below and started calling. No answer. Grabbing a flashlight from the captain's quarters, she raced from one spot to another. At last, in the stuffy forecastle, she saw a man lying on a bunk, his back to her. His hands and feet were bound.

"Captain Easterly!" she cried, turning him over.

Nancy loosened his bonds, then half dragged, half carried him to the foot of the companionway. She yelled for Bess and together they got him to the top deck. George was astounded to see him.

With a whiff of the fresh air, the captain finally regained consciousness from a hard blow he had received at the hands of Fred Lane. The scoundrel had tricked him aboard with the same kind of story which Fay had telephoned to the girls at the guesthouse.

"See here, what's going on?" the captain asked suddenly, realizing they were under sail.

Nancy told him what had happened. He tried to get up and help the girls, but he was too weak. It seemed no time at all before they were back in the safe waters of the little cove. Captain Easterly told the girls when to take in the sail and how to drop the anchor.

"We'll have to swim to shore," Nancy announced. "There's no boat."

The captain told them to be careful, and said he would be all right alone. George decided to stay with him, however.

Nancy and Bess quickly donned swimsuits and started off through the dark water. They were good swimmers and soon reached the beach.

Gasping and dripping, they rested a moment on the sand, then headed for the nearest house. Nancy asked the woman who answered her knock to telephone the police and ask someone to come there at once.

While waiting, the girls told the flabbergasted woman a little of the story. She lent them towels and gave each girl a beach robe to put on.

"Thank heaven you're safe," she said. "To think of such goings on in this quiet little cove!"

Nancy repeated her story to two troopers who arrived in a few minutes. They radioed an alert throughout the area, then set off in their patrol car in pursuit of the criminals.

Nancy borrowed a boat and returned to the clipper with Bess. They changed to street clothes, then with George and Captain Easterly came back to town. At headquarters they learned that Flip Fay and Fred Lane had been captured on the road to Boston. Fay had the ruby in his pocket and it was now in the possession of the police.

"The ruby won't cause any more trouble," said the real Mr. Ogden of the Eastern Shore Shipping Company, when he arrived the next day and met the group at State Police headquarters. "My company believes the ruby rightfully belongs to the descendant of Mathilda Witherspoon—Mrs. Smythe of Provincetown. What do you think, Mr. Farnsworth?" he asked the man who had inherited the clipper.

"I agree with you."

Nancy was delighted to hear this, knowing the woman needed money. "Oh, may I tell her?" she asked eagerly.

When Mr. Ogden nodded, Nancy sped to a telephone. The astounded Mrs. Smythe gasped.

When she got her breath, the woman asked Nancy to thank everyone, then added:

"When I told my neighbor about your coming the other day, she went to her attic and brought down a drawing of the *Dream of Melissa*. Maybe you'd like to have it."

Nancy was thrilled. "Is the figurehead on it?" she asked.

"Yes, indeed. She looks like she must have the day she first set sail."

"Thank you very much," Nancy said. "I'll get it tomorrow when I bring the ruby."

Red Quint, who was standing nearby, said he, too, had a present for Nancy. "I want you to have the snuffbox. You earned it, Miss Drew, catchin' up with a couple of pirates like Fay and Lane. You taught me a good lesson."

Nancy accepted the little carved box. She was relieved to learn that Red would probably be released on probation. Captain Easterly offered to take him on the clipper as a handyman and cook.

"That is," the captain added, "if I am going to have a chance to buy the clipper."

Mr. Ogden said he and Mr. Farnsworth had come to a gentlemen's agreement in the matter. The *Dream of Melissa* was to be deeded to Captain Easterly with a clear title! Mr. Farnsworth would receive a portion of the sale price.

"Then everything's settled," Bess sighed.

Nancy telephoned her father in River Heights and related the whole story. Carson Drew was overwhelmed to hear that so much had been accomplished in such a short time. Mr. Marvin's ring, Mrs. Marvin's jewelry, and the coins were found in The Crow's possession, and he had confessed to having overheard Nancy's plans by chance on the telephone during the robbery. Then he had gone to Boston to investigate the story of the *Bonny Scot,* in league with his buddy Lane.

After Nancy had discovered Fay on deck, and Captain Easterly had been sure he would not return, the thief had made two visits to the clipper and had hidden in the secret compartment below the wardrobe. From various vantage points, he had listened to Nancy tell Mrs. Smythe's story and had heard that a Mr. Ogden was coming from Baltimore. Fay had induced Lane to impersonate Ogden and take over the ship.

Fay himself had remained in town to spy on the girls. When he found out they had found Melissa, the thief changed his plans and tricked them into coming back on board. Had they left the figurehead behind, Fay would have stolen it from the guesthouse.

"Whew!" Bess sighed as she tucked herself into bed that night at the guesthouse. "I hope I never have such a day as yesterday in my life again!"

"Don't count on it," George yawned. "As long

as you're a friend of Nancy Drew, you'll run into exciting mysteries."

Very soon the cousins were to become involved with Nancy in *The Clue of the Black Keys*.

It was just two weeks after the girls had delivered the precious ruby to Mrs. Smythe that Captain Easterly gave a party on board his clipper. How different it looked! The ship had been painted a glistening gray. And set under the long prow was the figurehead, Melissa, restored and painted by Mr. Frisbie.

"Doesn't she look proud?" Nancy asked. "And look at the name on the ship!"

Painted in neat black letters across the stern was *Dream of Melissa*.

"The old pirate ship is gone forever," George said.

"And a good thing," Captain Easterly remarked. "I've even nailed up the secret passageway where that pirate Fay did his eavesdropping. What's more, this ship is going to be rechristened. And you know who's goin' to do the christening?"

Captain Easterly's blue eyes twinkled as he turned to Carson Drew and his daughter.

"Nobody but Nancy Drew!"

Eye a mystery . . .

Read **NANCY DREW** girl detective™

All-new stories in this *New York Times* bestselling series

Have you solved all of Nancy's latest cases?

Pit of Vipers

Getting Burned

Troubled Waters

Read them all!

The Orchid Thief

Close Encounters

Visit www.SimonSaysSleuth.com for a complete list of Nancy Drew titles, activities, a screensaver, and more!

Aladdin Paperbacks • Simon & Schuster Children's Publishing • A CBS Company
Nancy Drew © Simon & Schuster, Inc.

Chase Tornados and Culprits
as Nancy Drew® in
Trail of the Twister

Mystery Adventure Game #22

$100,000,000 is at stake in a competition to discover a formula to predict tornado touchdowns. But when equipment starts failing and crew members are injured, you as Nancy Drew, must join the team to keep them in the competition.

Is it just bad luck that's plaguing the storm chasers or is someone sabotaging their chances of winning?

dare to play™

Order at HerInteractive.com or call 1-800-461-8787. Also in stores!

Copyright © 2010 Her Interactive, Inc. HER INTERACTIVE, the HER INTERACTIVE logo and DARE TO PLAY are trademarks of Her Interactive, Inc. NANCY DREW is a trademark of Simon & Schuster, Inc. and is used under license. Copyright in the NANCY DREW books and characters are owned by Simon & Schuster, Inc. All rights reserved. Licensed by permission of Simon & Schuster, Inc. Other brands or product names are trademarks of their respective holders.

WIN MAC CD-ROM SOFTWARE

EVERYONE
E
Mild Violence
Comic Mischief
ESRB CONTENT RATING   www.esrb.org

Match Wits with The Hardy Boys®!

Collect the Complete
Hardy Boys Mystery Stories®
by Franklin W. Dixon

The Hardy Boys Back-to-Back

Celebrate over 70 Years with the World's Greatest Super Sleuths!

Match Wits with Super Sleuth Nancy Drew!

Collect the Complete
Nancy Drew Mystery Stories®
by Carolyn Keene

Celebrate over 70 years with the World's Best Detective!